THE BORED BRIDEGROOM

For as long as Lucretia Hedley could remember, she had loved the Merlyncourt estate and its handsome young lord, the Marquis. He was the most desired bachelor in all of Regency England and now, suddenly, she was to become the Marquis' wife and mistress of Merlyncourt.

But Lucretia knew the Marquis. She knew he had no patience for innocent, sweet girls. He would soon be bored with her and she would lose him.

Lucretia had to change. She was determined to become a woman—a sophisticated, experienced woman of the world. Little did she know that such a transformation would entrap both her and the Marquis in a chilling intrigue of danger and high adventure.

A spellbinding bestseller by the
world's best loved writer of romantic fiction
BARBARA CARTLAND

Books by BARBARA CARTLAND

Romantic Novels

The Fire of Love
The Unpredictable Bride
Love Holds the Cards
A Virgin in Paris
Love to the Rescue
Love Is Contraband
The Enchanting Evil
The Unknown Heart
The Secret Fear
The Reluctant Bride
The Pretty Horse-Breakers
The Audacious Adventuress
Lost Enchantment
Halo for the Devil
The Irresistible Buck
The Complacent Wife
The Odious Duke
The Daring Deception
No Darkness for Love
The Little Adventure
Lessons in Love
Journey to Paradise
The Bored Bridegroom

Autobiographical and Biographical

The Isthmus Years 1919–1939
The Years of Opportunity 1939–1945
I Search for Rainbows 1945–1966
We Danced All Night 1919–1929
Ronald Cartland
    (with a Foreword by Sir Winston Churchill)
Polly, My Wonderful Mother

Historical

Bewitching Women
The Outrageous Queen
    (The Story of Queen Christina of Sweden)
The Scandalous Life of King Carol
The Private Life of King Charles II
The Private Life of Elizabeth, Empress of Austria
Josephine, Empress of France
Diane de Poitiers
Metternich—the Passionate Diplomat

Sociology

You in the Home
The Fascinating Forties
Marriage for Moderns
Be Vivid, Be Vital
Love, Life and Sex
Look Lovely, Be Lovely
Vitamins for Vitality
Husbands and Wives
Etiquette
The Many Facets of Love
Sex and the Teenager
The Book of Charm
Living Together
Woman—The Enigma
The Youth Secret
The Magic of Honey

Barbara Cartland's Health Food Cookery Book
Barbara Cartland's Book of Beauty and Health
Men Are Wonderful

THE
BORED
BRIDEGROOM

Barbara Cartland

BANTAM BOOKS
TORONTO · NEW YORK · LONDON

THE BORED BRIDEGROOM
A Bantam Book / published May 1974

Library of Congress Cataloging in Publication Data

Cartland, Barbara, 1902-
    The bored bridegroom.

    I. Title.
PZ3.C247B03   [PR6005.A765]   823'.9'12   74-3488

AUTHOR'S NOTE

In May 1803, the Armistice between England and France came to an end. The news of the first British capture at sea on May 18th of two French ships threw Napoleon Bonaparte into a towering rage. He immediately ordered the arrest of all British travellers in France. Ten thousand were seized, some like Sir Ralph Abercromby's son as they embarked at Calais, others as they landed on French soil.

A baronet by delaying a few hours to enjoy the favours of an attractive Parisienne, found himself imprisoned for eleven years. Such internment of civilians was against all civilised procedure and convinced the English they were dealing with an untamed savage.

CHAPTER 1

1804

"Stay a little . . . longer!"

The voice was soft and pleading, but the Marquis somehow managed to extricate himself from a pair of close clinging arms and rose from the bed.

He stepped over a diaphanous gauze négligée which was lying on the floor, picked up his white neck-cloth and walked to the dressing-table.

He twisted the cravat round his neck and arranged it deftly with an expertise which would have surprised many of his contemporaries.

The woman watching him made no effort to cover her nakedness.

Lady Hester Standish was well aware—and she had been told so innumerable times—that her body was the acme of perfection.

Indeed, lying back against the lace-edged silk pillows and wearing only two strings of large black pearls, she was very beautiful.

Fair hair, blue eyes and white skin were prerequisites of beauty for the "Incomparables", toasted in the Clubs of St. James's, and Hester Standish eclipsed all rivals.

She was however at the moment not thinking of herself, which was unusual, but of the Marquis of Merlyn as he stood at her dressing-table with his back to her, his front reflected in the mirror.

She could appreciate at the angle from which she watched him the breadth of his shoulders, his muscular chest narrowing to a small waist above his slim hips.

He had an athletic body without an ounce of excess

flesh, and yet his manner gave so strong an impression of indolence that those who met him often wondered how he managed to keep so fit.

There was something about the Marquis, Hester Standish told herself, which made him irresistible to women. Perhaps it was the lazy look with which he regarded them.

His half-drooping eyelids, his habit of drawling, and most of all the mocking note in his voice which made it hard to be sure when he was serious or merely jesting, captivated them.

But while these things made him desirable, Lady Hester thought, it was really his elusiveness which incited females to pursue him relentlessly.

She watched the Marquis tidy his elaborately arranged hair, which had been fashioned in the windswept style set by the Prince of Wales, before she said:

"When shall I see you again?"

"We shall undoubtedly meet tonight at Carlton House," the Marquis replied. "It will be unbearably hot and a considerable crush. Why Prinny wishes to incur public criticism by such ostentatious hospitality in war-time I cannot imagine."

"His Royal Highness is bored with the war," Lady Hester pouted, "and so am I."

"That I can well believe," the Marquis replied. "At the same time this country is engaged in a desperate struggle for survival, and it will be many years before we know again the blessings of peace."

He was speaking seriously, but Lady Hester shrugged her shoulders petulantly.

The year before in 1803, when the Armistice with Napoleon had come to an end and England had declared war on the tryant, she had found it intolerable that the men who had knelt adoringly at her feet should suddenly be more concerned with serving their country.

The Armistice of 1801 which had given Napoleon time to build up his armies and plan his invasion had been treated by the English as an opportunity to disband half the Army and diminish the number of ships in the Fleet.

2

But the renewal of hostilities before the French were ready for it had galvanized the whole nation into activity.

Over 300,000 men joined the Volunteers who represented the whole nation. From the Duke of Clarence who commanded a Corps in Bushey to the lowest paid farm-worker, they were determined to a man to repulse the French if they landed on the South Coast.

"I told you all that childish hysteria last year was unnecessary," Lady Hester said now.

She recalled how infuriated she had been when her current lover had joined the Duke of Bedford as a private in their local Corps in which the Lord Chancellor had been a Corporal.

"Nevertheless it showed Bonaparte that we meant business," the Marquis replied, "and we may still be called upon to show our mettle if not prevented by idiots from doing so."

His voice was contemptuous. Lady Hester remembered that although he had pleaded to be allowed to rejoin his Regiment from which he had retired on his father's death soon after the signing of the Armistice, the Prince of Wales had forbidden it.

There had however been ways in which he could assist the war effort, and she wondered why, with his vast possessions and many interests, he should hanker after the Army.

"Are you never content, Alexis?" she asked suddenly.

"Content with what?" he enquired.

"With me for one thing," Lady Hester answered softly.

He stood at the end of the bed and looked down at her. It was hard to imagine any woman could be more delectable or more alluring.

"Come and kiss me," she whispered softly.

He shook his head, picked up his coat from a brocade-covered chair and shrugged himself into it.

Magnificently tailored it fitted without a wrinkle, and he looked so handsome now he was dressed that Lady Hester said again, and this time there was no

3

mistaking the note of passion in her voice:

"I want you to kiss me, Alexis."

"I have been caught in that trap before," the Marquis answered with an amused smile.

He knew from past experience that when a man bent over a woman lying on a bed and her arms went around his neck, it was easy for her to draw him down to her! And often impossible to escape!

"Goodbye, Hester."

She gave a little cry.

"Why must you leave me?" she asked. "George will be at Watiers the whole evening. When he left me at luncheon time his fingers were itching for the cards."

She paused and added beguilingly:

"I want you to . . . stay."

"You are very persuasive," the Marquis said, "but I have an appointment to keep."

"An appointment?" Lady Hester snapped the words and sat up. "Who is it? If it is another woman I swear I will tear her eyes out!"

"There is no need for such jealousy, if that is the emotion you are expressing," the Marquis drawled. "As it happens, it is my sister I am meeting."

"What does Caroline want that cannot wait?" Lady Hester enquired crossly.

"That is what I intend to find out," the Marquis replied. "So I must bid you farewell, Hester, and thank you for your kindness."

He walked towards the door and now Lady Hester sprang from the bed and ran towards him.

The sunshine coming through the windows which looked out onto Berkeley Square made golden patches on her white body and shimmered on the pale gold of her hair.

She was very alluring as she sped across the carpeted floor and reached out her arms towards the Marquis.

She drew his head down towards her.

"I love you, Alexis," she said, "I love you! And yet you always seem to elude me. Have you no tenderness for me?"

"I already told you," the Marquis said, "that you are the most attractive woman I know."

It was not the answer she wanted, but because she knew only too well she could not force him to make the protestations of love which she desired, she had to be satisfied with what he would give her.

Her lips parted, hungry for his kisses, were very near. Her eyes were half closed, her long lashes dark against the fragility of her cheeks.

"Kiss me," she begged, "kiss me."

And now there was a glint of fire in her blue eyes and her body was moving against his.

The Marquis kissed her without passion. Then when she would have clung closer still, he picked her up in his arms and carried her back to her bed.

He dumped her down against the pillows and with a note of laughter in his voice said:

"Try to behave with some propriety, Hester! If I cannot call on you tomorrow afternoon I will endeavour to be here on Thursday, unless George is at home."

"I cannot survive so long," Lady Hester replied dramatically.

But the Marquis merely laughed again and walking from the room, closed the door behind him decisively.

When he was gone Lady Hester made a little *move* with her lips at the door. Then with a gesture of irritation she flung herself back against her pillows.

It was always the same, she thought. When the Marquis left her she always felt afraid that she would not see him again.

She could never be sure of him, never be certain that he found her so irresistible that he must return.

Lady Hester would however have been slightly placated had she known that the Marquis's thoughts as he drove his Phaeton from Berkeley Square towards Merlyn House in Park Lane, were of her.

He found her amusing and he enjoyed the knowledge that he was in fact the only man for whom she had given up her other lovers.

Hester Standish had been unfaithful to her husband since the third year of their marriage.

She had been wed, almost as soon as she left the

5

schoolroom, to a good natured, wealthy peer who soon discovered that the ups and downs of gaming were more predictable than his wife's caprices.

Hester Standish had blossomed into a great beauty at the age of 25. Now at 28 she was undoubtedly sensational and at the same time insatiable for love.

She had caused innumerable scandals until she found it was wiser not to parade her lovers too obviously, because in the Society in which she shone it was a mistake to be ostracised by the women.

It was undoubtedly this new attitude of decorum in public which had enabled her to capture the Marquis for whom she had set every possible snare for over three years.

Since peace had come and he had retired from the Army, the Marquis had begun to enjoy the social world which opened its doors to him with alacrity.

It was not surprising that he was sought after.

He was not only one of the best looking men in the Beau Monde, he also had a proud title, vast estates, and the possibility of considerable wealth once his father's debts were settled.

The previous Marquis had been a gambler. He had frequented the clubs of St. James's, gambling in the company of Charles James Fox and other inveterate gamesters, until at times his family feared there would be nothing left of the huge fortune accumulated by their ancestors.

But fortunately an early death had brought his son the title and saved the majority of family treasures.

But if he had not owned a penny-piece, the Marquis would still have been pursued by lovely women. And he would have been a fool, which he certainly was not, if he had not been aware of his own attractions.

He had realised that Hester Standish was chasing him, and he had deftly, without appearing to do so deliberately evaded her with a skill and agility which had driven her nearly frantic.

Finally he had succumbed to her wiles because she genuinely aroused his desire, and also because he wished to discover for himself if her much vaunted attractions were exaggerated.

He thought now, as he tooled his horses in the manner which had gained him quite rightly the honour of being an acknowledged Corinthian, that Hester was perhaps the most passionate woman he had ever met.

She was insatiable, and although the Marquis was noted as a lover of such experience that he could arouse almost any woman to the heights of passion, he sometimes thought Lady Hester outpaced him.

"She is very beautiful," he told himself, and knew even as he said it that he was not in the least in love with her.

She attracted him, he desired her, but he was aware that their most ardent and erotic love-making never involved his heart.

"For what am I searching?" he asked himself with a twist to his lips.

He remembered another woman almost as beautiful as Lady Hester and a leader of society who had asked him almost the same question.

She had lain in his arms and the room had been mysterious with shadows from a dying fire. There was a fragrance of tuberoses and the Marquis had reflected drowsily how comfortable he felt and how at peace he was with the world.

Then the woman with her head on his shoulder had said:

"What are you seeking, Alexis?"

"What do you mean by that?" he asked, surprised at the question.

"I know that however much I love you there is always some part of you which I cannot reach," she answered. "I feel invariably that I somehow fall short of the ideal—if that is what it is—that lives deep in your heart."

"That is absurd!" the Marquis had answered tenderly. "You are everything I want, everything I could expect to find in a woman."

Yet even as he spoke he had known that he lied.

Lovely, delectable, desirable as the woman was, perfect though their love-making seemed, she was right when she had said she was not enough.

It was the same with Hester Standish. No woman could be willing to give more of herself, and he knew that he excited her as no other man had even been able to do before.

Their eyes had only to meet across a crowded room for them to be aware that something magnetic stirred within them. The flame of desire flickered and would at the touch of each other grow red-hot, rising burningly to consume them both.

And how beautiful she was!

The Marquis smiled to himself as he remembered all the little mannerisms by which she continued to draw attention to her body.

Black pearls against her white skin, the blue garters she would wear embroidered with her initials in diamonds.

The manner in which sometimes she would greet him wearing nothing but a pair of coloured slippers or on another occasion, two enormous diamond earrings which fell almost to her shoulders.

There was no allurement that Lady Hester was not prepared to utilise if it would captivate the attention of a man and make him realise his need for her.

And there was no doubt, the Marquis decided, that when it became an obsession such as she had for him, it was very gratifying.

At the same time, as he reached his house in Park Lane and drew up his horses outside the pillared portico, he decided he would not call on her tomorrow!

He walked into the marble Hall noting with satisfaction that the Van Dykes he had just been able to purchase back after his father had sold them looked magnificent in the afternoon sunshine.

"Is Her Ladyship here?" he asked the butler.

"Yes, M'Lord. Her Ladyship is waiting for Your Lordship in the Blue Salon."

The Marquis walked upstairs to the first floor. The Blue Salon was an impressive room, its white and gold

8

walls a perfect background for a collection of pictures by French Masters.

There were however several empty panels and the Marquis's expression darkened whenever he noticed them. But now he had eyes only for his sister who was standing at the window looking down into the garden.

"Alexis!" she exclaimed as he entered the Salon, "I had begun to think you had forgotten about me."

"You must forgive me for being late, Caroline," the Marquis answered. "I was unavoidably detained."

"And I can guess who detained you," the Countess of Brora said with a smile.

She was five years older than the Marquis, and while she was an attractive woman her looks were not so outstanding as his.

Nevertheless elegantly dressed in what he realised was a new Spring bonnet and carrying a large muff, Caroline Brora could still hold her own with the majority of society beauties.

"I was just thinking," she said as she walked towards the sofa, "that the daffodils will be out at Merlyncourt. You know how fantastic they are in the spring, and as it is so warm for this time of year, they will already look like a glorious golden carpet as one comes down the drive."

Her brother looked at her with an amused expression in his eyes. Despite his appearance of laziness there was little that escaped the Marquis. Now he said:

"I have the feeling, Caroline, you have come to speak to me about Merlyncourt."

"I have indeed," she answered. "How did you guess?"

"You are very transparent, my dear," the Marquis replied. "I had hoped you wished to see me for myself."

"You are also involved in what I have to say," the Countess replied.

Then putting her muff on the sofa beside her she said:

"Have you any idea what is going on, Alexis?"

"About what?" he enquired.

"What Jeremy is doing?" his sister replied.

"Jeremy!" There was a sharp note in the Marquis's voice. "I paid his debts only a month ago, he cannot have run through what I gave him so quickly! If he has—then this time he can damn well go to a debtors prison."

"It is not money," the Countess replied, "at least not directly."

"Stop talking enigmatically, Caroline," her brother commanded, "and come to the point. What has Jeremy done to perturb you?"

The Countess of Brora drew in her breath.

"He is boasting, and I am sure with reason, that he intends to marry Lucretia Hedley."

For a moment the Marquis looked blank, and then he said:

"Hedley? Do you mean . . . ?"

"I mean," his sister interrupted, "the girl who lives with her father in the Dower House, who now owns not only the house which has belonged to us for generations, but 500 acres of land in the very centre of the estate."

She paused for breath and then she continued:

"Do you realise what this means, Alexis? You will have Jeremy sitting on your doorstep. You will have him boasting that he owns a part of Merlyncourt. He thinks that already! But if he marries this girl he will be a continual thorn in your flesh, you cannot deny that."

"I would not attempt to deny it," the Marquis said. "Why was I not told of this before?"

"Because you never show interest in anything that goes on in the County," his sister replied. "And I have been North with William."

She looked at her brother pleadingly as she said:

"Alexis, you cannot allow this to happen! You know it was a disaster that Papa ever allowed that Hedley man to purchase the Dower House and to live right on top of us. That was bad enough! But to have Jeremy there!"

There was a note of horror in the Countess's voice and the Marquis was not surprised.

They both disliked their cousin Jeremy Rooke who was Heir Presumptive to the Marquisate and who had managed not only to commit every crime in the Social calendar at one time or another, but also to be perpetually in debt.

The Marquis had saved him from prison so many times that he had lost count. And his sister declared openly that she now would not even acknowledge Jeremy if she met him in the Park.

There were no depths to the depravity to which Jeremy would sink, and no financial skulduggery in which he would not indulge.

The Marquis was well aware that his sister was not exaggerating when she said that to have him living on the Merlyncourt estate would create a situation which would be intolerable.

"Tell me exactly what has happened," he said and his voice was quiet in contrast to the almost hysterical note of Caroline's.

"It was the Duchess of Devonshire who told me about it as soon as I arrived in London," she began, "and then I asked various of our other friends about him and they all told me the same story. Jeremy has been boasting everywhere that he will be in possession of 500 acres of Merlyn land and be an extremely rich man."

"I know of course that Sir Joshua Hedley is wealthy," the Marquis said slowly.

"He is enormously rich," the Countess ejaculated, "there is no doubt about that! And the girl is young. I suppose she does not realise what Jeremy is like, or perhaps they crave an even closer link with Merlyncourt."

The Marquis did not speak and his sister cried:

"How Papa could have done anything so stupid as to sell the Dower House, I shall never know!"

"I think the inducements and the price paid for it made it worth his while," the Marquis answered.

"I remember how upset I was at the time," the

11

Countess of Brora continued. "I wrote to you and although your reply was not very eloquent, I am certain you felt it as deeply as I did."

The Marquis did not answer. He walked across the Salon to look out of the window. Caroline was right. The spring sunshine would bring out the daffodils at Merlyncourt, and the house would have a fairy-like beauty as it was reflected in the silver lakes.

"Damn it!" he said aloud, "I will not have Jeremy leering at me behind every tree, walking over the place as if he owned it."

"He will own a part of it," his sister said bitterly.

"How could this girl—whatever she is like—be beguiled into marrying a man like Jeremy?" the Marquis enquired.

"I do not suppose it is her wish," his sister replied, "it will be her father who is arranging it all. After all it was he who persuaded Papa to make such a fool of himself, and I suppose to those who do not know him as we do, Jeremy is a matrimonial catch. If you do not marry, he will be the 5th Marquis of Merlyn."

There was silence for a moment and then the Marquis said:

"I assure you, Caroline, I have no intention of allowing Jeremy to inherit."

The Countess gave a little cry and rose from the sofa.

"Oh, Alexis, that is exactly what I hoped you would say! That is of course the solution, but I was so afraid that you would not agree to it."

"Agree to what?" the Marquis asked in surprise.

"To marrying this girl yourself! Can you not see it is the perfect solution?"

"Marry who?" the Marquis asked, although he knew the answer.

"Lucretia Hedley!" his sister answered. "I have made enquiries and I am told she is quite attractive. And whatever we may think about Sir Joshua's behaviour, the girl is well bred. After all her mother was a Rathlin."

12

"It must have been a mésalliance for the daughter of a Duke," the Marquis remarked.

"Nonsense!" his sister contradicted. "I am sure the Duke was delighted at the chance of having a wealthy son-in-law. The Rathlins, like most rich families, were always on the verge of bankruptcy, and as it happens I have always heard that Lady Mary Hedley adored her husband. Anyway she is dead now, and what is important is that the girl has good blood in her."

There was silence from the Marquis and his sister continued:

"The Hedleys were North countrymen, but they were gentlefolk, and when Sir Joshua inherited vast plantations in Jamaica it was to be expected he would marry into the nobility."

The Marquis walked back from the window to stand beside his sister.

"Are you really suggesting that the only way we can prevent Jeremy moving into the Dower House is that I should marry this girl? It is a crazy idea!"

"Is it so crazy?" Caroline Brora enquired. "You have to marry someone, some day. You have to beget an heir, unless you are prepared to see Jeremy step into your shoes! After all this is the only way we can get back the Dower House and 500 acres."

"In exchange for my freedom," the Marquis said with a little twist to his lips.

"In exchange for kicking Jeremy off the estate," Caroline Brora retorted. "When I think of the way that man has behaved, when I think of the things he has said and the things he has done, I cannot tolerate the idea of seeing his horrible face peering at me through the bushes at Merlyncourt!"

The Marquis laughed and it was a sound with no humour in it.

"You hate him, Caroline."

"I loathe and detest him!" she said. "But you must admit that on this occasion he is being clever."

"In what way?" the Marquis enquired.

"Well for one thing, in finding an heiress. Do not forget Lucretia Hedley is an only child and I have learned on good authority that Sir Joshua gets richer every year."

The Countess of Brora's voice deepened:

"I am told that according to Jeremy the marriage settlement will be somewhere in the neighbourhood of £500,000."

"Good God!"

Even the Marquis seemed for a moment shaken out of his indolent manner.

"That is a fortune is it not, Alexis?" Caroline Brora went on, "and a fortune you could well employ. There are still several pictures missing from this room. The silver plate is still on sale in Bond Street."

She made an exasperated ejaculation.

"I think that jeweller keeps it in his window just to annoy me. I always cross the road before I come to the shop!"

Then looking at her brother she said more softly.

"And as far as you are concerned, Alexis, the stables are half empty, your hunting-box in Leicestershire has been let for the last three years, and I can think of a dozen other things for which you need money. Certainly £500,000 pounds will warm your pockets."

"You sound like all the temptations of St. Anthony rolled into one," the Marquis retorted.

His sister made a little gesture.

"How else can I persuade you that this is your duty, not only to yourself, but to us, the family who love Merlyncourt and cannot bear Jeremy to defile even one inch of it."

"I must think," the Marquis said slowly.

"There is no time for that!" his sister cried. "Jeremy is boasting all over London that his betrothal is to be announced at any moment."

"There is always the chance of course," the Marquis said slowly "that my charms even if I employ them, will not outweigh Jeremy's. The girl might be in love with him."

His sister made a sound which in anyone less well-bred would have sounded suspiciously like a snort.

"Really, Alexis, how can you talk such fustian!

14

You know as well as I do that a girl—any girl—would much prefer a Marquis, whatever he may be like, to Jeremy Rooke. And if with your much vaunted charm you cannot persuade one stupid ignorant little school-girl to fall in love with you, then I despair!"

She smiled and added:

"After all you have had a great deal of practice with much more experienced hearts!"

"Much more experienced!" the Marquis agreed. "Good God, Caroline, can you see me saddled with a school-girl? What on eearth should I say to her?"

"She may be a school-girl at the moment . . ." Caroline Brora began, then paused before she continued. "As a matter of fact I think she is older than that. She spent last winter at Bath and was in London for a short time last season."

"I see you have all the answers," the Marquis said. "Suppose you now tell me exactly what you do know about this wench."

"I made it my business to find out about her," the Countess replied. "She is attractive, I am told, but unfortunately, where you are concerned, she is a bru-nette."

She glanced at her brother mischievously as she spoke, and then she added:

"Your *penchant* for blondes, dear Alexis, is well known. Let me see—shall I innumerate your loves over the past ten years? There has been Lady Jersey, the Duchess of Devonshire . . ."

"That is enough, Caroline."

The Marquis's voice held a note of authority which his sister did not dare disobey.

"You tell me the girl is a brunette," he said quietly. "Continue."

"You will remember of course that the Duchess of Rathlin, Lady Mary's mother, was French," Caroline Brora went on. "That accounts of course for the girl having dark hair. But I believe that otherwise she is quite appealing. She has been well educated, Sir Joshua has seen to that, and after all she should have some

15

of her father's brains. You may dislike him Alexis, as I do . . ."

"You appear to forget I have never met him," the Marquis interrupted. "We decided—or you decided—when our father died that we would not know the Hedleys, since we were justifiably incensed that they had persuaded Father into a course of action of which we all thoroughly disapproved."

"Yes of course I remember," the Countess said hastily, "but I met Sir Joshua when Papa was alive. He is a good-looking man and surprisingly cultured. In fact if there were a choice, I would prefer to have him living in the Dower House rather than Jeremy."

"That goes without saying," the Marquis replied. "As far as I can ascertain they have been no trouble since they have lived there—except of course that Hedley is prepared to pay higher wages and employ more men on his farms than I could ever afford."

"That will all be changed when you marry Lucretia," his sister observed.

"You seem to be convinced that I will agree to your mad scheme," the Marquis remarked resentfully.

His sister threw out her hands.

"What alternative is there?" she enquired. "Except to let Jeremy have his way and invade Merlyncourt."

"God damn him! I will not stand for that!" the Marquis ejaculated.

"I thought you could not bear it any more than I can," Caroline Brora said. "And now let me inform you, Alexis, there is no time to be lost. You must offer for the girl immediately. Otherwise there is no doubt that Jeremy, who is no fool, will whisk her up the aisle too quickly for you to prevent it."

The Marquis's lips tightened, and his sister with a sense of satisfaction realised by the squareness of his chin that he was determined to prevent his Cousin's audacious plan being successful.

She put out her hand and laid it on his arm.

"I am sorry, Alexis," she said, "that you should have to marry anyone with whom you are not in love. But you know as well as I do, dear brother, that you

16

spend very little of your time in social circles where you are likely to meet young girls."

"I was well aware that I would have to marry one day," the Marquis replied, "but I can assure you, Caroline, that at the moment the idea bores me to extinction!"

CHAPTER 2

"The acceptances are pouring in!" Elizabeth said excitedly. "Everyone in the County is coming and it will be even a bigger Ball than Mama gave for my sister Anne."

"Papa was telling me what a splendid occasion that was," Lucretia smiled.

"We shall have over 500 guests," Elizabeth enthused. "But of course the bored Marquis has refused."

"The Marquis of Merlyn?" Lucretia enquired.

"Your neighbour!" Elizabeth replied. "I hoped he might come, but I might have guessed that a party of this sort would be beneath his condescension."

"I wonder why," Lucretia remarked.

"I can tell you if you want to know," Elizabeth said.. "Mama was very anxious he should attend Anne's Ball! I think she thought he would make Anne a suitable husband! Anyway when he refused the invitation, she instructed my brother Henry to speak to him at his Club."

"What did he say?" Lucretia asked curiously.

"He said," Elizabeth replied, " 'My dear Henry, if there is one thing which bores me it is unbroken horses, immature wine and unfledged girls!' "

Lucretia laughed.

"I am sure there was nothing your brother could reply to that."

"Nothing," Elizabeth agreed, "and Mama was furious! After all Papa is Lord Lieutenant and of considerable consequence in the County, and one would

18

have thought the Marquis might have been more obliging just for once."

"But your mother has been magnanimous enough to
ask him for the second time," Lucretia suggested.

"It is not magnaminity, if that is the right word,"
Elizabeth replied, "it is because she hopes that he
might take a fancy to me! Poor Mama, she always was
over-optimistic!"

"Why should he not do so?" Lucretia asked. "After
all, Elizabeth, you are very pretty."

"But definitely unfledged," Elizabeth said wrinkling
her nose. "Besides I would be terrified! I assure you I
have no wish to marry the bored Marquis. Can you
imagine anything worse than to have a husband who
continually yawns in one's face?"

Elizabeth paused before she said reflectively.

"Nevertheless, he will have to marry some time,
otherwise that odious Jeremy Rooks will inherit Merlyncourt!"

As Elizabeth finished speaking she put her fingers up
to her lips.

"Oh, I forgot he is a friend of yours! Do forgive
me!"

"He is no friend of mine," Lucretia answered. "Papa
keeps asking him to stay. I cannot think why. In fact
I do find him quite odious."

Her friend Elizabeth looked at her speculatively out
of the corners of her eyes.

"Do you really mean that, Lucretia?"

"Yes, of course I do," Lucretia replied. "Why should
I lie to you?"

Elizabeth hesitated for a moment. Then she said:

"I suppose you know that everyone is talking about
you and Jeremy Rooke."

"About me!" Lucretia exclaimed. "Why even to
speak of him gives me goosee pimples! He is so suave
and smarmy! Besides I am certain that he is as crooked
as a cork-screw."

Elizabeth threw back her head and laughed.

"Lucretia, you do say the most incredible things!
But I do agree with you in this instance, and there are

certainly far more attractive men at your feet than the nauseating Jeremy Rooke."

Lucretia did not answer, and after a moment Elizabeth said shyly:

"Are you in love with any of them, Lucretia?"

"If you mean those red-faced boys and leering middle-aged Don Juan's who have one eye on me and another on my fortune," Lucretia replied, "the answer is no!"

Elizabeth looked at her wide-eyed.

"Do you really think they are more interested in your money than in you?"

Lucretia smiled and Elizabeth went on:

"But that is ridiculous! You are so lovely and so clever! I am really sure that every man who meets you loves you for yourself."

"You are very flattering and very sweet," Lucretia said, "but I have inherited some of Papa's hard business sense, and I assure you, Elizabeth, I often question if I had no money at all how many admirers I would have left!"

"Dozens and dozens," Elizabeth said loyally, "but certainly not Jeremy Rooke!"

The two girls laughed.

"Well one thing is certain," Elizabeth said, "no-one will marry me for my money, not with three brothers, two sisters, and poor Papa frantically avoiding the Duns."

"And yet your father can afford to give a ball for 500 guests," Lucretia exclaimed.

"That is a sprat to catch a mackerel," Elizabeth retorted, "and I am the sprat! After all, Anne got married to Lord Bolton in her first season and they have great hopes for me."

"And you do not mind the idea of marrying someone you hardly know?" Lucretia enquired, "just because your father and mother arrange a suitable match?"

Elizabeth shrugged her shoulders.

"What alternative is there," she asked, "except to sit at home and become an old maid? In a year's time,

20

when Belinda is seventeen, she will have her Ball and if she married before me I swear I would die of shame."

Lucretia started to say something, then changed her mind.

Instead she said goodbye to her friend and leaving the Earl of Munster's impressive if somewhat shabby residence, drove her smart curricle drawn by a fine pair of chestnut bloodstock back home.

As she travelled down the country lanes where the hedgerows were just beginning to put forth the first green buds of Spring, Lucretia looked pensive.

She had few girl friends of her own age and she was fond of Elizabeth, but she realised they had no tastes in common.

The idea of any woman being pitchforked into the competitive marriage market was to Lucretia extremely distasteful and she could not understand Elizabeth's placid acceptance of it.

She was still thinking of Elizabeth and the huge and expensive party that the Earl and Countess of Munster were giving for her and which they could ill afford, when she passed the wrought-iron gates of Merlyncourt.

She glanced through them and had a quick glimpse of the great house exquisite in the Spring sunshine with its silver lakes encircling it like a necklace.

Then as she drove on she realised that above the grey roof amongst the twisted chimney-pots a flag was flying.

This meant that the Marquis had come home and was in residence!

"I wonder why he has returned?" Lucretia thought.

She answered her own question by imagining that perhaps he was giving one of his gay parties which invariably caused a spate of ill-natured gossip in the County—principally because the local gentry were not invited to them.

It was only half a mile down the road when Lucretia turned in at a smaller gateway which led to the Dower House.

Nevertheless the heraldic lions which were part of

21

the Merlyn crest surmounted tall stone pillars on either side of the gates, and the Merlyn coat-of-arms was emblazoned on the walls of both lodges.

The Dower House which had been built in the reign of Charles II was by no means as impressive as Merlyn-court, but still a very beautiful mansion.

The additions and improvements which Lucretia's father had made to the house had doubled its size and also made it extremely comfortable as well as exceptionally luxurious.

Lucretia drew up her curricle outside the front door and handed the reins to the groom.

"Thank you, Ferris," she said with a smile.

"Will you be riding this afternoon, Miss?" the man enquired.

"I expect so," Lucretia answered. "Bring the horses round at two o'clock."

"Very good, Miss."

The groom touched his hat and a footman hurried down the front steps to help Lucretia alight. She walked into the beautiful raftered hall with its curving oak-carved staircase and huge marble chimney-piece.

"Sir Joshua is in the library, Miss," the butler told her.

Lucretia walked quickly to the library door and entered the room to find her father seated at his desk.

He rose to his feet when she appeared and she lifted up her face to kiss him affectionately.

"Did you buy the horse you wanted?" she asked.

"I bought three," he answered. "I think you will approve of them. One I am certain is a winner."

Lucretia smiled.

"If you win any more races, the Jockey Club will warn you off all race-courses," she teased. "You are too successful, Papa!"

"I flatter myself that my success at anything I undertake is due to careful planning and proper organization," Sir Joshua replied.

As he spoke he walked across the room to the window.

He was an extremely handsome man with strong

clear-cut features. His hair was just beginning to turn grey, and this gave him a distinguished look he had not had in his youth.

He was well dressed and everything about him proclaimed success and wealth. Yet he was far too clever to be ostentatious and far too cultured to show anything but good taste.

"I want to talk to you, Lucretia."

"Something has happened!" she exclaimed. "What is it?"

She was so close to her father and they had meant so much to each other since her mother's death, that she knew every intonation of his voice and every expression on his face.

Now she took off her riding-coat, threw it carelessly on a chair and untied the silk ribbons which had held her small flower-trimmed hat on her head.

She put the hat on top of the coat, then walked to the window to join her father.

He stood looking at her. Then he said:

"You are very lovely, Lucretia, and, as you know, I have always wanted the best for you in life."

"You have always given me the best," Lucretia smiled.

"I have tried to," her father answered. "And now I believe that something I planned for you many years ago is about to come to pass."

"You planned for me!" Lucretia echoed in surprise. "What can that be?"

"Your marriage!" Sir Joshua answered.

Lucretia stared at him in astonishment. Then she said:

"Did you say my . . . marriage?"

"Yes, I did," Sir Joshua replied. "Sit down, Lucretia, I want to tell you about it."

Almost automatically Lucretia obeyed him.

Sitting in the cushioned window-seat she looked at her father in bewilderment. Her eyes were wide and puzzled, as if what he had just said were the last words she had ever expected to hear from him.

For a moment Sir Joshua seemed to hesitate. Then he said slowly:

"You will remember when I bought this house four years ago, both you and your mother were surprised that I should have chosen a small estate in this particular part of the country, when I could have afforded something very much bigger and more impressive."

"Yes, I remember Mama talking about it," Lucretia said. "I remember too at the time you said you specially wished to live here. But you never told us why."

"I chose this house because it belonged to Merlyncourt," Sir Joshua answered.

"And you were close friends with the late Marquis," Lucretia interposed. "I think he was very fond of you, Papa."

"He was fond of what I could give him," Sir Joshua said. "He was a gambler, Lucretia, and a gambler often needs rich friends.'

"You mean you gave him money?" Lucretia exclaimed.

"I lent him money," Sir Joshua corrected.

He was silent for a moment and Lucretia said:

"So that was how you persuaded him to sell you this house and the land which for generations had belonged to his family."

"Yes, that was how it was done," Sir Joshua said frankly. "And I also included in the deal two horses of mine which the Marquis particularly envied. One which you may remember won the Derby, the other was extremely successful at Newmarket. They would have done better still if their owner had not sold them."

"But why did you do all this, Papa?" Lucretia asked.

"Because, my dearest," her father answered, "I wished you in time to become the Marchioness of Merlyn."

"You wanted me to marry the present Marquis?" Lucretia asked.

"I realised that he was a very presentable young man. He had breeding, he also had the position in life that I would wish for my daughter. What was important too, was that he was liked by other men."

24

Lucretia looked out into the garden.

"I can hardly believe, Papa," she said quietly, "that you planned this all those years ago. I was only fourteen at the time!"

"Fourteen, but still my only daughter. The person whom next to your mother I love best in the world."

"But how is it possible, however much you love a person, to choose a husband for her?" Lucretia said. "For one thing, I might dislike the Marquis, whom I have never met, and for another thing I am quite convinced, Papa, that he would have no wish to marry me."

"That is where you are wrong," Sir Joshua said. "I have been clever—very clever, Lucretia!"

He spoke with an almost boyish satisfaction which Lucretia knew well.

It was one of the most endearing qualities about her father that he could not resist boasting a little of his achievements.

He longed for her applause and approval when he brought off a clever deal, discovered a treasure for the house, or sent one of his carefully thought out schemes soaring to success!

Lucretia could not help smiling at him as she said: "What have you done, Papa?"

"When I decided that you should marry the present Marquis, I was well aware that he might be difficult," Sir Joshua began. "He has, as you well know, a reputation for being very gay and for moving in the sophisticated Society which centres round Carlton House. A Society which would certainly not welcome in its midst a young girl of your age!"

"I have heard that myself," Lucretia murmured, remembering the conversation she had had only a short while ago with Elizabeth.

"I therefore knew that if the Marquis was to become your suitor," Sir Joshua went on, "I would have to play my cards very carefully."

"What cards?" Lucretia enquired.

"I had two trumps," Sir Joshua replied with a twinkling in his eyes. "My first was money, my second was Jeremy Rooke!"

"Jeremy Rooke!" Lucretia exclaimed. "Whatever has he to do with it?"

Sir Joshua laughed. It was a chuckle of a naughty, mischievous little boy.

"Only that I have made very certain that the social world and the Marquis himself believes that you are about to announce your engagement to the Heir Presumptive to the Marquisate."

"Elizabeth told me this morning that people were talking about us!" Lucretia exclaimed. "Papa, how could you do anything so preposterous? You know I would rather die than marry Jeremy Rooke!"

"And I would rather see you in your coffin than married to such an unutterable swine!"

Lucretia looked at her father in astonishment as he went on:

"But what you and I feel about Rooke is very mild compared with the feelings of his family. I know that the Marquis has paid up his debts not once, but dozens of times! I know that the Countess of Brora loathes the very sound of his name! Not one of his relatives has a good word for him!"

He paused to finish impressively:

"And that is why, my dear, the idea of his lording it here at the Dower House is, I was convinced, more than they could possibly stomach!"

"So you think that to save me from Jeremy Rooke, the Marquis will propose to me himself!" Lucretia cried. "Papa, it is the most absurd notion I have ever heard in my life!"

"Not so very absurd," Sir Joshua replied, "for I have just half an hour ago, received a letter from the Marquis. He has asked to see me on a matter which he is sure will concern us both very deeply."

"He said that?" Lucretia asked incredulously.

"He wrote it in his own hand," Sir Joshua replied. "Do you realise, Lucretia, it is the first time he has ever so much as acknowledged my existence!"

He laughed.

26

"Oh, I was well aware what I was doing when I persuaded the old Marquis, because he owed me so much money and because he wanted more, that the only way he could repay me was to let me have this house and 500 acres! This to the Rooke family is sacred ground, of course it antagonised them."

"And you thought it did not matter?" Lucretia asked.

"I knew it was of no consequence," Sir Johua replied. "I was here, I was in possession, I was on the doorstep! However much the young Marquis might refuse to meet me, he could not forget me. Then, when I met Jeremy Rooke, I realised that fate had played into my hands."

"He also wanted money I suppose?" Lucretia asked sarcastically.

"Not only wanted it, he was desperate for it!" Sir Joshua replied. "But I was not over-generous where he was concerned. A little here—a little there! The real carrot I held out was the thought of marriage with my only child who would receive a stupendous dowry as a bride and my whole fortune when I was dead."

"Go on," Lucretia spoke quietly, but she was very pale.

"I knew the idea would be abhorrent to the Marquis and to his family," Sir Joshua said, "and you see, Lucretia, as usual I was correct in my assumption. The Marquis has come to me! I shall see him this afternoon, and I am prepared to wager any sum you like to name that he will offer formally for your hand in marriage."

Lucretia rose to her feet and walked to the fireplace to stand with her back to her father.

She did not speak and he sat in the window-seat watching her, his eyes on her bent head.

After a moment he asked softly:

"You are angry with me, Lucretia?"

"I hate to think of being used in such a way," she answered. "Manipulated is perhaps the right word. I loathe the idea of being married to a man who wants

27

my money, my home, but is not the least interested in me!"

"And do you think any man could really separate you in his mind from your background and your possessions?" Sir Joshua asked.

Lucretia remembered what she had said to Elizabeth, and after a second she answered miserably:

"Do you really believe, Papa, that no man could . . . love me for . . . myself?"

"I think many men will love you, my dearest," Sir Joshua answered. "But you have to remember that rich though I am, noble though your mother was by birth, we still do not havee the entrée into the Society where I would wish you to shine! You are too young for one thing, and for most women the pass-key to the social world must inevitably be marriage."

"I would . . . wish to . . . fall in love," Lucretia said in a low voice.

"That is what all human beings want," Sir Joshua answered. "But do you really think you could love any of the men you have already met? I have watched you, Lucretia, refuse many suitors. Some of them have pleaded with me. Many more have approached you, and I know you will agree when I say that not one of them has been worthy of you."

"And the Marquis?" Lucretia asked. "Do you really think that he will be caught in the trap you have set for him?"

"He is already in it!" Sir Joshua answered. "Either he has to face the possibility of his cousin whom he detests and despises living here and owning part of the Merlyncourt Estate, or else he has to step in and prevent the marriage. How else can he do that except by offering for you himself?"

"But he has never . . . met me," Lucretia said weakly.

"And he was never likely to do so, unless I had taken the initiative," Sir Joshua retorted.

He paused before he went on:

"I had hoped, Lucretia, that by some lucky chance we would come into contact with the Marquis, or per-

28

haps his sister, while we were living here. But I realised, as soon as the old Marquis died, that they intended to ostracise me. I had offended them by supplying the money their father needed so urgently, and the fact that I obtained anything in exchange only heightened my crime."

"It was a most unfair decision on their part, Papa," Lucretia said hotly.

"No, I can see their point of view," Sir Joshua answered. "I have learnt not to expect gratitude, and you know as well as I do, Lucretia, that most people do not like the very rich—they are merely envious of them."

"That sounds very cynical, Papa."

"It is common sense to face facts," Sir Joshua replied, "and that is why, Lucretia, I am asking you as a very intelligent young woman to face them. You can go on as you are, being pursued by the rag-tag and bob-tail of the County, hoping that sooner or later a man will come along who has just enough wealth for you to deceive yourself into believing that it is your face and not your fortune he is after!"

Sir Joshua's voice sharpened. Then he said:

"Yet I hope you are wise enough to see your position dispassionately and realise that you were meant for better things! Could you really tolerate a hard-riding, hard-drinking nincompoop merely because he had a title? Could you really listen night after night to inanities from a man whom you despised both for his lack of intellect and culture?"

"And you think I shall admire the Marquis?" Lucretia asked.

"I am certain of it!" her father replied. "For one thing he was outstandingly brilliant at Oxford. For another I myself have heard him praised by the Commanding Officer of his Regiment and by Lord Wellington."

His voice rose as he continued:

"The Prince of Wales, who is no fool when it comes to artistic appreciation and learning, values his friendship as much as that of Charles James Fox. That is significant, Lucretia! Clever men seek the company of their peers!"

Sir Joshua made a gesture with his hand as he went on.

"What is more, though you may not think it important, the Marquis is a sportsman. He is an acknowledged Corinthian and as popular with the hoi-polloi on the race-course as with the members of the Jockey Club."

"You paint a very attractive picture, Papa," Lucretia said with a hint of irony in her voice.

"When you meet the Marquis this afternoon you will realise I am not exaggerating," Sir Joshua said.

"You are so certain that I will accept this outrageous scheme of yours!"

Lucretia turned from the fire-place and walked back to stand beside her father looking down at him.

"I am relying on you to use your ingenuity," he answered quietly, "something you have always done up to now, Lucretia. And after all, let us be frank, you and I, your heart is not involved elsewhere."

He smiled beguilingly as he said:

"If it was, I promise you I would not force you to do anything which was really at variance with your desires."

"And if I . . . agree?" Lucretia asked faintly.

"Then I shall inform the Marquis that you are prepared to accept his offer of marriage."

"You are so sure . . . so completely sure that . . . this is what he . . . intends," Lucretia murmured.

"I have already offered you a wager on it," Sir Joshua reminded her.

Lucretia looked out into the garden. The April sunshine was for the moment obscured by clouds. There was a promise of rain, and a sharp wind had sprung up to scatter some of the almond blossom from the trees that encircled the green lawns.

Then across the grey sky there was a sudden flight of white doves. They appeared from between the trees and vanished over the roof of the house.

Exquisitely beautiful it seemed to Lucretia there was

almost a symbolic message in the flutter of their wings and the swiftness of their flight.

Slowly, almost as if she forced them, the words came to her lips.

"Very well, Papa, I will agree to what you . . . suggest. But I will not be . . . here this afternoon, I am going to London."

"To London!" Sir Joshua ejaculated.

"Yes, Papa. I wish to buy some clothes to make the very best of myself before I meet the Marquis. You understand?"

Her father's eyes searched her face.

"Do you think that is wise, Lucretia?"

"I think what I intend to do is very wise," Lucretia answered. "Will you trust me, Papa, as I . . . trust you?"

He smiled at her and his eyes were tender.

"You are all I have to love in the whole world," he answered. "I am grateful to you, Lucretia, for trusting my judgement in what I know is the most momentous decision of your life. I cannot be so ungracious to forbid you to do anything which you think is right."

Lucretia took a deep breath.

"Tell the . . . Marquis," she said and it seemed almost as if her voice trembled on the words, "that I am deeply aware of the honour that he does me. Arrange for the Marriage to take place the last week in May and make sure, Papa, he does not press to see me until I return."

Sir Joshua rose to his feet.

"What are you up to, Lucretia?"

"You are to ask no questions, Papa! I will let you in to my secret a little later. In fact no-one shall know about it but you. But I have no intention of letting the Marquis see me as I am now."

"But why? What does all this mean?" Sir Joshua enquired.

Lucretia lifted up her face and kissed her father on the cheek.

"You will learn about it all in good time," she said. "Please do as I say, the rest I leave to you."

Then before her father could speak she had gone from the room and he heard her voice giving orders for a travelling-carriage to be brought to the door.

Upstairs Lucretia did not ring immediately for her maid, but walked to the long mirror which stood against one wall of the very lovely and exquisitely decorated bedroom.

In front of it Lucretia stood staring at her reflection.

She saw herself as if she was a stranger, noticing first the very large eyes which seemed for a moment almost unnaturally bright as if they reflected some inner excitement.

They were beautiful eyes, Irish eyes, "blue set with dirty fingers" as tradition went. But the colour was not the pale translucent blue which was so admired amongst the young girls who would attend Elizabeth's Ball.

It was a dark tempestuous blue, the blue of the sea before a storm.

Lucretia's hair was raven black, and swept back from her oval forehead its darkness was echoed in the winged eye-brows that had a beauty all of their own.

It was a very lovely face with its straight little nose and soft full mouth, and yet Lucretia looked at herself despairingly. She was thinking of the Marquis's avowed taste for fair women like the Duchess of Devonshire and Lady Hester Standish.

It was understandable, living on the very door-step of Merlyncourt that she should have heard all the gossip about the most noteable, handsome and sought after young man in the whole of the *Beau Monde*.

And she thought now that instinctively, yet unconsciously she must have been aware of her father's machinations ever since they had come here.

She remembered feeling an excited curiosity about the Marquis from the very moment she had stepped into the Dower House and seen the roofs of Merlyncourt peering above the trees.

She had slipped away by herself and climbed through the woods which lay behind the house to where from what she afterwards thought of as her "look-out," she could see below her Merlyncourt in all its glory.

She had known then as she drew in her breath, at the beauty of it, that it would always mean something in her life, something she could not escape.

The Marquis had been away from home with his Regiment, but it seemed to her as if no-one talked of anyone else.

The servants in the house, the workers on the estate, all chattered about the "young Master," until finally on his father's death he in his turn became "The Master."

Lucretia had learnt of his pranks when he was a child, of his escapades as a young man, of his love affairs as he grew older.

Because she was curious she had deliberately invited a most garrulous gossip to tell her more.

She had heard Mrs. Munns, the House-keeper at Merlyncourt almost crippled with rheumatism was ill and had persuaded her mother to let her take the woman some special healing herbs.

After Lady Mary died, Mrs. Munns had believed she was doing a real kindness in letting the poor motherless girl from next door come frequently to Merlyncourt for a cosy chat.

She had no idea how often Lucretia manufactured an excuse to call and ask her advice, only so they could talk together of the Marquis and his latest exploits.

And there were other people too—the game-keepers, the foresters, the grooms, all of whom had tales to tell of the Marquis when he was young.

When they began to repeat themselves and there was nothing more to learn from them, Lucretia as she grew older found that the Marquis was the favourite topic amongst the County families.

There were younger men, who met him in London and made veiled hints about his amorous exploits, while girls like Elizabeth, sitting silent at family meals, listened with "big-ears" to the morsels of scandal related by their parents.

Lucretia had known that Lady Hester Standish was

hunting the Marquis almost as soon as he knew it himself.

When they finally became lovers, the news flashed through the County as swiftly and deviously as the flight of a woodcock.

Lady Hester had long been a subject for pursed lips and frequently expressed disapproval. But no-one for a moment argued about her beauty.

"The loveliest creature on whom I have ever set eyes!" Lucretia heard the Earl of Munster announce one day at luncheon.

"Her behaviour is disgraceful," the Countess remarked acidly.

"What can you expect with every man in St. James's dangling after her and laying their hearts at her feet?" the Earl retorted.

The Countess sniffed and he continued:

"Even at my age I cannot help enveying young Merlyn! She'll lead him a hell of a dance, but I am prepared to bet my last shilling it'll be damn well worth it!"

"Really Robert, in front of the girls!" the Countess protested frigidly.

"Sorry, me dear, sorry!" the Earl replied.

Lucretia had listened with wide eyes. And now staring at her own reflection in the mirror she realised she was the exact opposite in appearance to the much-acclaimed Lady Hester.

How could she compete with her dark hair and stormy eyes with the golden pink and white perfection of the most beautiful woman in England.

"I have not a chance," Lucretia whispered miserably to herself.

Then something proud and determined within her made her lift her chin high. She would not be defeated so easily. She would not surrender without a struggle.

She walked to the window. In the distance there was just a sight of one of the Merlyncourt chimney-pots above the trees.

He was there! He had come home, and if her father

34

was to be believed it was because he intended to ask for her hand in marriage!

"I have to try to win him," Lucretia said to herself. "I may not be the type of beauty he admires, I may not be sophisticated, but I have one thing which perhaps some of his other women have lacked, and that is brains!"

She turned sharply from the window and crossed the room to pull the bell which hung beside her bed.

She pealed it half a dozen times. Then as her maid came hurrying, wondering what had occurred, she said commandingly:

"Pack half a dozen gowns, not too many, because I intend to buy new, but just enough for the first few days I shall be in London. We are leaving now! Now immediately!"

"Now Miss!" her maid exclaimed. "But I must have more time!"

"There is no time to argue," Lucretia said. "Get the housemaids to help and pack your things as well. We are going to London, Rose, and it is an important journey! Perhpas the most important journey I have ever undertaken."

CHAPTER 3

Lucretia on arriving in London drove to Sir Joshua's house in Curzon Street.

Although she was not expected everything was in readiness, as there was always a full complement of servants there, as well as in the country.

Sir Joshua had also arranged for an elderly cousin of Lady Mary's to live in the house, so that she could chaperone Lucretia whenever it was required.

Lady Byng was a widow and employed her time most enjoyably in playing cards and gossiping with her cronies.

There were three of them seated round a baize-covered card-table when Lucretia entered the Drawing-Room.

Lady Byng rose to her feet in astonishment.

"Lucretia!" she exclaimed, "I was not expecting you. Your father told me you would be staying in the country for at least another week."

"Do not let me disturb you, Cousin Alice," Lucretia begged, "I have to go out again almost immediately. I will tell you all my news when I return later this evening."

"That will be delightful, my dear," Lady Byng replied.

She was an obliging chaperone in that she seldom asked questions and was, Lucretia knew, only curious when she felt she could sense a scandal.

Lucretia greeted the other elderly ladies round the card-table with the flattering good manners which she knew would make them speak of her when she had left as 'that nicely behaved young woman'.

"It is time you got married, Lucretia," one of them said coyly. "I am expecting to hear the peal of wedding bells any day now!"

Lucretia smiled, but when she would have answered, Lady Byng interposed:

"The trouble with Lucretia is that she has too many Beaux. It is the girls who have only one who make up their minds quickly."

"That is true," another old lady sighed. "When I was young I had a dozen gallants at my feet with the unfortunate result that finally I chose the wrong one."

They all laughed at this and Lucretia made her escape.

Upstairs Rose heleped her change into an elaborate evening gown and arranged her hair. Lucretia bedecked herself with more jewellery than she usually wore.

Finally, wearing a velvet cloak trimmed with ermine, she went downstairs to find, as she expected, Sir Joshua's town carriage waiting for her.

The red carpet was rolled across the pavement, but instead of stepping into the carriage, Lucretia looked up at the Coachman resplendent in his livery and gold braided hat.

"Did you get the information I required, Marlow?" she asked.

"Yes, Miss Lucretia. I understand the players are at the Haymarket Theatre."

"Thank you, Marlow. Will you take me to the Stage Door?"

Lucretia stepped into the carriage and the Coachman who had been with the family for some years looked at the Butler with consternation.

Never in all the time he had driven Lucretia had he received such a strange order.

Servants however did not query the actions of their employers, however eccentric. The footman shut the door and climbed up behind the carriage to stand on the swaying platform at the rear looking extremely smart with his powdered hair, plush knee-breeches, cockaded hat and crested-buttons.

The horses, which many gentlemen walking in the street looked at in admiration, carried Lucretia along Piccadilly, through the Circus and down the street which in the last few years had grown from a country lane infested by footpads at night into a busy thoroughfare.

Sir John Vanborough who had built Blenheim Palace had designed the Play-House on the corner of Pall Mall which had become the Royal Italian Opera House.

Almost opposite it was the Theatre Royal, Haymarket, the oldest but one of all the theatres in London.

It had battled, Lucretia knew, through many vicissitudes including many dismal years after it was first built when it could not obtain a licence.

And yet in one way or another it had always managed to survive, and many great actors had proclaimed their lines from its stage and brought in audiences who appreciated them.

Lucretia had been taken by her father to see many of the plays which had been performed at the Theatre Royal. Only the previous year she had seen a new comedian, Charles Matthew, who had played in *The Jew* and *The Agreeable Surprise* with such success that the King and Queen had come to see him three times in the first fortnight.

However no play, however successful, ran for long, and Lucretia was not surprised to learn that now in the interval before the next production the Theatre had been let to 'The St. Petersburg Players'.

This was the company in which she was particularly interested.

She and her father had paid a visit to Bath the previous winter. They were there only a short time because Sir Joshua had found that the Spa bored him, and also he disliked several of the young men who were paying court to Lucretia.

But during their visit Lucretia had been entranced by the acting of the company who styled themselves 'The St. Petersburg Players'.

The play itself had not been particularly distinguished, although dramatically effective. But she had been extremely impressed by the ability of the actors.

"Surely they are outstanding," she had remarked to one of her friends in Bath.

"It is to the man who produces them," was the answer. "He is, I understand, a quite exceptional person called Ivor Odrowski. From what I have heard he is somewhat of a mystery, but he certainly understands the theatre."

There was one woman in the cast whose acting Lucretia had never forgotten. She played the part of a seductress luring the hero to social destruction. Yet she had done it so subtlely, conveying the character not only by her words, but in the look of her eyes, in the movements she made, in the shrug of a shoulder or a faint gesture of her hands.

It had been, Lucretia had thought at the time, art personified, and the actress's performance had remained in her mind long after she had left Bath.

The carriage drew up outside the Theatre and Lucretia realised that she would have to walk to the Stage Door which was situated down an alley-way at the side of the building.

Accordingly, with the footman escorting her, she passed through the crowd perambulating up and down outside the theatre and found a short distance down the alley, an unimpressive entrance through which the actors and actresses would enter and leave the theatre.

There was an old white haired porter sitting inside the door.

"I wish to speak to Mr. Ivor Odrowski," Lucretia said.

"He won't see ye, M'am," the man answered surlily. "He don't have no visitors before a performance, ye'll have to wait 'til after 'tis over."

Lucretia glanced at the footman who understood what she expected of him and produced a coin from his pocket which he slipped into the old man's hand.

"Well I'll see what I can do," he said grudgingly.

Rising to his feet he disappeared into the darkness of the narrow passage.

It all seemed, Lucretia thought, somewhat gloomy and very different from the bright garish opulence in the front of the theatre.

There was a smell of damp and dust, greasepaint and ale which she felt must have hung about the passages ever since the theatre had first been built.

A woman, gaudily dressed with a painted face and quite obviously dyed hair, came in from the street.

"Where's Ben?" she asked loudly and to no-one in particular.

Lucretia was just about to reply when the old man returned shuffling down the passage.

" 'ere, what do ye want?" he asked of the newcomer.

"You knows what I wants," the woman replied. " Will he see me?"

"There's an audition tomorrow, ten o'clock sharp," Ben answered.

"Well I 'opes I'm lucky this time," the woman said. "If there 'aint too many others trying for the part."

She gave Lucretia an insolent glance, looked at the young footman with a half smile and went out again into the alleyway.

"He'll see you, Ma'am," Ben said to Lucretia.

"Thank you," Lucretia answered and followed the old man down the passage.

It was dark and Lucretia felt that the floor was also greasy with dirt. They climbed a narrow staircase to the first floor and after passing several doors, the old man opened one with only a perfunctory knock.

"Th 'lidy to see ye, Sir."

Lucretia passed by him into a small square dressing-room.

She had never been in a stage dressing-room before, yet it was exactly as she had expected.

Plush curtains, a hard red-velvet couch, a dressing-table littered with sticks of grease paint, lotions, salves flowers, good-luck tokens, half empty glasses and the butts of several cigars.

A wardrobe stretching the whole length of one wall
40

had its doors open and she could see a mass of gaudy costumes. They had almost a forlorn look about them as if without a human aid they had lost confidence in themselves.

Everything was shabby and untidy and the carpet across which the occupant of the dressing-room advances to greet her was threadbare.

"Ben told me that you wished to see me," a voice said. "He was so insistent that I should do so that I have broken my rule never to entertain before I perform."

"I am most grateful," Lucretia replied. "My name is Lucretia Hedley and I wish to see you on business."

Mr. Odrowski was an arresting looking man and she remembered now that he had played a part in the play she had seen at Bath. She had not realised then who he was.

He was flashily handsome with dark hair drawn back from a square forehead. His features were clear cut, although his full sensuous mouth seemed somehow at variance with the hard expression of his eyes.

He spoke with a pronounced accent, and Lucretia wondered how he found it possible to play any part on the stage save that of a foreigner.

She realised with a faint amusement that Mr. Odrowski was taking in every detail of her appearance. She was aware that it was the ermine on her cloak and the jewels glittering in her ears and round her neck besides the tip which had impressed Ben and procured her the interview.

"Will you not sit down, Miss Hedley?" Mr. Odrowski asked. "And may I offer you any sort of refreshment?"

Lucretia shook her head.

"Thank you, but as I feel we have very little time before the curtain rises, I would like to come straight to the point."

"That is acceptable to me," Mr. Odrowski said. "So tell me in what way I can serve you. I cannot believe you wish for a part in one of my plays."

His eyes flickered once again towards Lucretia's jewels.

"Not exactly," Lucretia answered.

She paused for a moment and then began.

"I saw your play when I was at Bath last winter. I was extremely impressed, not so much by the play itself, but by the acting of your players."

"That would have been *The Wronged Wife,* would it not?" Mr. Odrowski inquired.

"I think that was the name," Lucretia agreed. "But what I remembered particularly was the performance of the actress who played the seductress."

"Miss Kelly!" Mr. Odrowski exclaimed. "She is an excellent actress."

"I was told that her ability really rested on you," Lucretia said. "That it is your direction and the manner in which you produce your players which makes them so outstanding."

"You flatter me, Madam," Mr. Odrowski smiled.

"Is it flattery to tell the truth?" Lucretia asked.

"In which case I can only say thank you."

"What I have come to ask you," Lucretia went on, "is to teach me to act in the same manner as Miss Kelly."

Mr. Odrowski looked at her sharply.

"I regret, my dear young lady, that I have no part at the moment available for someone like yourself. In the short season we are here, we are giving a very different type of play to *The Wronged Wife.*"

"I have told you that I do not require a part on the stage," Lucretia answered. "What I am asking, Mr. Odrowski, is that you should coach me privately. I do not propose to become a professional actress, but I wish to be taught how to act."

Mr. Odrowski smiled.

"I have had many strange requests in my time," he said, "but never one quite like yours. I am sorry, Miss Hedley, but I must refuse. You are very lovely, and it would have been a pleasure to instruct you, but frankly I have not the time."

"I think one can always find the time for anything

that one wants to do," Lucretia retorted. "I am aware, Mr. Odrowski, that your time is expensive. I am also quite sure you sometimes find it difficult to finance your new productions."

She saw a sudden glint of interest in the Actor's dark eyes and she went on:

"Shall I be quite blunt and say that in return for your services I am prepared to finance your next theatrical venture, whatever it may be."

For a moment Mr. Odrowski stared at her incredulously and then he said:

"Have you any idea what that could cost you?"

"It is of little consequence," Lucretia said. "My father is a rich man and he has no objection to my spending his money in any way I wish. What I suggest is that I write you a draft now for half the moneys you will require and for the other half when my lessons are complete."

Mr. Odrowski walked across the dressing-room.

"This is an extraordinary proposition, Miss Hedley, so extraordinary that for the moment I am lost for words. I will not pretend to you that we are not in need of money. Who in the theatrical world ever has enough?"

He made an expressive gesture before he continued:

"But what you are asking me to do may prove impossible. You are an amateur, you are also a Lady of Quality. You may be impossible to teach, I do not know. But even if I am successful, you would be paying me too high a fee."

"That is for me to decide," Lucretia answered. "I am prepared to pay for your services, Mr. Odrowski, because I believe that what you can teach me will be of tremendous benefit to me personally. If I asked a man to give me a diamond bracelet, you would not be surprised. What I am asking you to give me is something which I consider far more valuable. I mean your creative ability to make me—a young woman—appear a sophisticated woman of the world."

Mr. Odrowski threw out his arms in an exaggerated manner.

"But why should you ask such a thing? You are young, you are lovely, you are adorable as you are! What man could resist such freshness, such instinctive elegance? To me you are as entrancing as Spring, a young girl on the threshold of life. What could be more alluring?"

"Men have varying tastes, Mr. Odrowski," Lucretia said.

The Actor glanced at her sharply.

"Then this is an *affaire de coeur.*"

"If you mean that my heart is involved," Lucretia answered, "the answer is yes. Perhaps that will make me a better actress, I do not know. All I say is that it is imperative for me to appear to be sophisticated, and to this end I am prepared to leave myself entirely in your hands. I want you to show me how to walk, how to talk, how to smile, and most of all how to dress."

Again the Actor turned to stare at her almost incredulously, and then he said:

"Is this true what I am hearing? For if it is, I find it a fascinating proposition. I am not only interested in the money, Miss Hedley, that goes without saying. But as a producer, as a dramatist, as a man who loves acting for acting's sake, then I can imagine nothing more thrilling than to change a vision of budding Spring into the voluptuous blossom of Summer."

He stood looking at her for a moment. Then he said:

"Take off your cloak."

She obeyed him, undoing the clasp and letting it fall from her shoulders onto the floor.

Her dress was very fashionable. Of white gauze it was embroidered with seed pearls and frilled round the hem and round the décolletage with lace.

It was elaborate and expensive, but it was a young girl's gown. It had come from one of the most famous shops in Bond Street, and Cousin Alice had helped Lucretia choose it for a Ball at which she had never lacked a queue of partners for every dance.

But Lucretia knew, as the Actor stared at her, that even with the glitter of diamonds round her neck and

44

in her ears, no-one would mistake her for anything but a young and unfledged girl.

There was silence, and after a moment she asked anxiously:

"Can you do it?"

"Walk across the room," he commanded.

She did as she was told without self-consciousness.

"I like the way you move," he said, "but it is very English!"

Lucretia laughed.

"I was afraid that was what you would think, and yet actually I am a quarter French."

"Mon Dieu, but that is excellent!" the Actor exclaimed in French. "I will be honest with you, Mademoiselle, my father was French and my mother was Russian. But because the French are not—what shall we say—very popular at the moment, I have reversed my ancestry."

"Very sensible!" Lucretia commented.

"And also The St. Petersburg Players have a delightfully exotic sound about them, have they not?"

"The romantic unknown," Lucretia laughed.

"I will teach you in French," the Actor went on. "It is a language which comes easier to my lips than English, and it is the language of sophistication."

He made a sound of derision and continued:

"It is only the English to make such a fetish of youth! The French prefer experience. A woman in France will be courted until she is in the grave, but not in England. Oh no! By the time she is forty, they are talking about her as old, old! *Mon Dieu!* what a hideous word!"

Lucretia laughed.

"I shall be happy to become sophisticated in any language," she said. "The only thing is, we have very little time, Monsieur."

"How long?"

"Three weeks."

He threw up his hands.

"C'est impossible!"

"Nothing is impossible," Lucretia protested, "not

45

when you have a pupil who is willing to work as hard as I am."

"Very well," he said, "it is agreed! But I shall make you work until you drop. My players will tell you I am a hard task-master—even when we have time to rehearse and they already know their lines."

"I am not afraid."

Lucretia crossed the dressing-room and sat down at the table glittered with grease paints.

"I have brought with me a Bankers draft," she said. "Will you tell me what sum you require?"

Mr. Odrowski hesitated for a moment. Then he named a figure which, while large, Lucretia knew was not exorbitant for financing the production of a new play.

She wrote quickly in her neat upright hand and signed her name with a flourish.

Then she turned to smile at the man who was watching her.

"When do we begin?" she asked.

"What are you doing now?" he enquired.

"I have no plans for this evening," she replied, "and I was hoping I could watch this performance. Afterwards I would like if it is possible and you have no other engagement, to invite you out to supper."

The Actor smiled.

"What about your reputation, Mamselle?"

"We can take someone with us," Lucretia replied, "or better still eat where we cannot be seen. But there again I must leave myself in your hands."

"You are very trusting," he said slowly. "How do you know that I will not seduce you? You are a very desirable young woman."

"Firstly I am capable of looking after myself," Lucretia answered, "and secondly I cannot believe that as an ambitious actor-manager you would find any woman worth the loss of the draft which lies on your dressing-table."

Mr. Odrowski threw back his head and laughed.

"I like you and I admire you!" he said. "It will, I assure you, Miss Hedley, be a pleasure to teach you, and I have a feeling that it will not be a very difficult task. In fact I may be earning all that money under false pretences."

"That is a risk I am prepared to take," Lucretia said. "But let me assure you, Monsieur, that if you are a hard task-master, so am I. I, also, will only be satisfied with perfection. I not only have to be word-perfect in my part, but it also has to be fool-proof. I must not be detected. I have to deceive experts."

"Or surely you should say one connoisseur," Mr. Odrowski said perceptively.

"I stand corrected," Lucretia smiled at him.

"I salute you, Mademoiselle!"

He took her hand as he spoke and raised it to his lips.

Instead of the perfunctory kiss that was customary, his lips lingered for a moment on her skin and Lucretia knew even as he did so that it was in the way of a test.

She smiled at him in what she hoped was an alluring manner, and as he raised his head to look into her eyes, she knew she had not been mistaken.

"Look at me through your eyelashes," he said. "Drop your eyelids a little and look up. That is better. Now smile faintly—not a grin, just a twist at the corners of your mouth. That is better! Much better! Now slowly, very slowly, as if you are loth to do so, take your hand from mine."

She did as she was told.

"Good!" he exclaimed. "Now I am going to find out if there is a free box in the front of the house. But you realise, Mademoiselle, that you cannot sit there alone."

"I hoped you could find someone to sit with me," Lucretia replied.

"But of course," Mr. Odrowski agreed. "I myself can be with you for the first Act. For the second, when I appear in a small part, I will send one of my young men with instructions to play the gentleman. If he does not do so convincingly, you will tell me afterwards where he was at fault."

He picked up Lucretia's cloak from the ground as he spoke and put it over her shoulders.

She reached up her hands as he did so to take the clasp.

"No!" he said sharply, "you should have turned your head slightly towards me. There is no hurry, you hope that my hands will linger on your shoulders. Now turn your head, showing the length of your neck. Your eyes look up into mine and your eye-lids flutter a little. That is better. Not really perfect, but better. And now walk very slowly to the door moving your body from the hips."

Lucretia obeyed him.

"Look back at me and smile," he commanded, "faintly, not too ingratiatingly. The kind of secret smile that a woman gives a man when they have an understanding between them. This is good! Quite good!"

He nodded his approval and went on:

"Now you wait for me to open the door, and when you walk ahead of me down the passage you remember all the time I am looking at the back of your head. You want me to think of you, so you think yourself into my consciousness. Do you understand? It is not only what you do, Mademoiselle, it is what you think and what you feel."

He paused for a moment as if he wanted her to remember his words, and then he said quietly:

"Perhaps what you feel will be for you the easiest part of all."

In the country Sir Joshua found himself looking again and again at the clock on the mantelshelf as it drew near to the time that he had suggested to the Marquis he should call.

He decided after some thought that he would receive his guest in the Library. It was so essentially a man's room, while the Salon, which had been decorated by his wife, seemed somehow too ornate and too feminine.

Accordingly when the Marquis of Merlyn was announced, Sir Joshua was sitting at his desk making, he was aware, quite an impressive picture of industry with a pile of papers in front of him and a white quill-pen in his hand.

He rose immediately to his feet and walked towards the Marquis his hand outstretched.

He had often seen the Marquis in London at the various clubs of which they were both members, and he was therefore not surprised by his handsome appearance or by the fact that the Marquis was one of the best dressed men in the whole of the *Beau Ton*.

It was not only the fact that his clothes were well designed and perfectly tailored. He had also an aptitude for wearing them which made them so much a part of himself that they actually became a frame for his personality.

Sir Joshua was aware that the Marquis's expression was serious and his grey eyes had a slightly steely glint in them as he walked across the room to take his host's hand.

"It is kind of you to see me, Sir Joshua," he said in a deep voice which seemed somehow characteristic, "at such short notice."

"Your letter sounded urgent and naturally it made me curious," Sir Joshua answered.

"At the same time," the Marquis said, "I feel I owe you an apology. You have lived here for nearly five years, Sir Joshua, and this is the first time we have met."

Sir Joshua indicated a comfortable wing-backed armchair by the fireplace.

"Will you not sit down, My Lord," he said, "and may I offer you a glass of wine—or brandy if you prefer it?"

"A glass of wine will be very acceptable," the Marquis replied.

The Butler had remained just inside the door waiting for instructions. Now he left the room to return almost immediately with a footman carrying a large silver salver on which were various crystal decanters and engraved wine glasses.

The Marquis accepted a glass of claret, Sir Joshua

49

helped himself to some brandy. The servants withdrew and the two men faced each other across the hearth-rug.

"You have made this room very charming," the Marquis said.

"I hope I may show you the rest of the house later on," Sir Joshua replied.

There was silence for a moment and then the Marquis began:

"Have you any idea, Sir Joshua, why I have asked to see you?"

The older man smiled.

"I naturally have speculated on what the reason could be," he replied, "but I have never been fond of guessing-games. I would rather you told me."

"Then I will be frank, Sir Joshua, and say that the reason I am here is because I have decided it is time I was married."

"That is the explanation I rather expected," Sir Joshua said quietly.

"You, perhaps better than anyone else, the Marquis went on, "understand my financial position at this present moment. I am in the process of paying off what remains of my father's debts, and they should be cleared within the next two years."

"They were a heavy burden for any young man to inherit," Sir Joshua remarked.

"I think really I should thank you for the help you gave my father," the Marquis said, speaking as if the words were somewhat of an effort.

"I do not expect gratitude," Sir Joshua remarked, remembering he had said much the same words to Lucretia, "but your father might have had worse friends to turn to in desperation. Money-lenders would have extorted crippling usury for the loans."

"I am aware of that," the Marquis said, "and therefore I can only offer you my thanks. That is something I should have done a long while ago."

Sir Joshua did not answer and the Marquis, again with perceptible difficulty, continued:

"I understand that your daughter is now at a marriageable age. You already own a part of Merlyncourt estate. It seems to me eminently sensible that our families should be united."

"I agree with you," Sir Joshua answered.

"And your daughter?" the Marquis enquired.

"She is prepared to leave the decision in my hands," Sir Joshua replied. "She is an intelligent child and we have a very close relationship between us. You will not be surprised, My Lord, that I think that in marrying Lucretia you are a very lucky man."

"That of course goes without saying," the Marquis agreed. "Shall I have the pleasure of meeting your daughter this afternoon?"

"I am afraid not," Sir Joshua answered. "Lucretia is in London and she will not be returning for a week or so. She has, however, intimated that should it meet with your Lordship's approval she would be prepared for the marriage between you to take place at the end of May."

Sir Joshua paused a moment and went on:

"After that the season will be ending and most of our friends will be leaving London for the country. I imagine too that the Prince of Wales will go to Brighthelmstone."

"The end of May would suit me admirably," the Marquis said. "Your daughter would wish to be married in London?"

"I think that would be the most convenient for everyone concerned," Sir Joshua replied.

"In that case I shall not be surprised if the Prince does not offer us Carlton House for the wedding reception," the Marquis said. "He has always been a very good friend to me, and unless it was against your wishes, if His Royal Highness makes such a proposition, I should like to accept it."

"I should of course be extremely honoured," Sir Joshua remarked.

"Shall I tell my Attorney to get in touch with you as regards the Marriage Settlement?" the Marquis enquired.

"I think a Marriage Settlement on your part would

be rather unnecessary," Sir Joshua replied. "As you must be aware, Lucretia is a very large heiress. I have already settled a great deal of money on her, and her husband will have the handling of it from the day she marries. On my death my entire fortune will become hers."

The Marquis inclined his head.

"I have moreover," Sir Joshua said, "something to show you which I think you will find interesting. It will in fact be my wedding-present to you personally."

He rose to his feet as he spoke, and with the Marquis following him, Sir Joshua led the way from the Library through the Hall and down a long passage beeautifully furnished which led, the Marquis realised, to the new additions to the house.

They had been so skilfully carried out that to someone who had not known the Dower House in the past it would be hard to perceive where the original building ended and the new additions began.

They were perfectly in keeping, the rooms decorated with ancient panelling, their ceilings painted in the same manner which made the originals at Merlyncourt so outstanding.

And everywhere the Marquis noticed there were pictures, furniture and ornaments which with his experienced eye he recognised as being not only valuable but often priceless.

Finally, after what seemed a long walk, they reached a large mahogany door which Sir Joshua opened and the Marquis followed him into a long narrow room with windows overlooking the garden.

"This room has never been used," Sir Joshua said quietly, "because I have kept it as a store-house for the presents I intended to give you on your marriage."

"To give me?" the Marquis asked almost incredulously.

"No-one else would appreciate them quite so fully," Sir Joshua replied.

The Marquis looked round him. The walls were hung with pictures rising one above each other right up to the ceiling. The furniture was arranged round the walls and in the centre of the room. And he realised as he stared in bewilderment that he recognized every piece.

There was the inlaid marquetry chest that his father had sold ten years ago when he could not meet the bets he had laid on the Thousand Guineas race at Newmarket.

There were the bronzes that had gone the following Christmas after a wild evening at Watiers at which he had lost over twenty thousand pounds.

There on the walls were the French pictures from the Salon at Merlyn House, and the Raphael which had always stood in the Chapel at Merlyncourt! The Rubens which had hung in the Banqueting Hall was also there beside a Holbein of Henry VIII.

The Marquis turned round and stared at another wall. Yes, he recognised everything from his childhood! Even the gold framed chairs which had been made for Merlyncourt when Queen Anne had stayed there and which he remembered had vanished without an explanation.

"You bought them all," he said at length.

"All except the Van Dykes which I understand you have already recovered," Sir Joshua replied. "I realised that your father was about to deplete Merlyncourt and I could not bear it to happen."

"You could not bear it?" the Marquis enquired. "What do you mean by that?"

"I travelled a great deal after inheriting an enormous fortune from my uncle's estates in Jamaica," Sir Joshua answered, "and everywhere I went I found some great beauty which thrilled me and which remained in my memory long after I had left the country or place where I had seen it. Then, one day, soon after I was married, I saw Merlyncourt."

He paused before he explained.

"One of my carriage-horses cast a shoe on the Dover Road, and because it irked me to hang about waiting for a blacksmith, I had a saddle put on one of the other horses and told my servants I would ride for half an hour so as to get some exercise."

Sir Joshua stopped speaking as if recalling what had happened, before he continued:

"It was quite by chance that I saw Merlyncourt, and I knew at that moment I had never seen anything so beautiful anywhere else I had been in the world."

"I agree with you," the Marquis said, "but I am prejudiced."

"To me Merlyncourt represented everything that was perfect in England," Sir Joshua said, "and because I have always been audacious, I rode up to the front door and asked to see the Librarian."

"The Librarian?" the Marquis ejaculated in surprise.

"I concocted some story that I had found a book in my library which I felt belonged to yours," Sir Joshua continued. "The Librarian was not unnaturally interested and we talked for some time. Inevitably we discovered our interests in common and he showed me the house. It thrilled me as nothing had ever thrilled me before."

Sir Joshua looked at the Marquis as he said slowly:

"It was when I returned to London I learnt that your father was intent on despoiling a unique treasure collected over many generations."

"You can imagine what we felt," the Marquis said bitterly.

"And you hated me when you learnt that I was buying your family treasures," Sir Joshua smiled. "What you did not know was that I persuaded your father, once I had met him through an introduction in the Club, to sell me anything on which he found himself having to raise money."

"I wish I had known," the Marquis said.

"I would not have dared to confide in you because you were so young," Sir Joshua answered. "I knew your pride would be hurt. But your father had very little pride. When he wanted money I lent it to him! Only when he was ashamed to ask me for more and was determined to sell something, did I force him to sell to me rather than to outsiders."

"We are greatly in your debt," the Marquis murmured.

"I do not want you to feel that," Sir Joshua said. "I was not thinking personally of you. Beauty is something none of us can buy, and for which none of us can pay. When the collection in this room is returned to you the day you marry, think of it not so much as a gift to yourself, but to the generations that will come afer you—your children, your grandchildren, and their children who will love and cherish Merlyncourt as I an outsider loved it."

There was a touch of emotion in Sir Joshua's quiet voice which the Marquis found strangely moving.

He looked round the room once again, and then without waiting for Sir Joshua walked without speaking back to the Library.

Then as Sir Joshua joined him and the eyes of the two men met, the Marquis held out his hand.

"I am very honoured, Sir Joshua," he said, "that our two families should be joined together."

"I might say the same," Sir Joshua answered, "but instead I will ask just one thing of you—be kind to Lucretia."

"I will show her the respect that is hers automatically in the position of my wife," the Marquis answered.

It was a cold answer, but somehow he felt himself incapable of saying more. Sir Joshua however seemed satisfied.

When the Marquis drove away, tooling his horses down the drive and along the road back to Merlyncourt, he found himself thinking of Sir Joshua with a warmth that had certainly not been in his mind a few hours earlier.

He liked him. There was no doubt about it, he liked his future father in law and was deeply grateful to him, which was something he had never expected to be.

The he remembered Lucretia and felt a feeling of restriction and anxiety about the future.

Sir Joshua was one thing, his daughter was another!

"What in God's name," the Marquis asked himself, "have I got in common with a girl of eighteen?"

He was convinced that what he had arranged was the right thing, but he could not help feeling a deep depression seep over him at the thought of being married to a very young girl, however pleasant she might prove on acquaintance.

He thought of all the women he had known—women either his own age or only a few years younger—and he knew, however much he might try to pretend that marriage was the only solution to the problem of Jeremy Rooke, that every instinct in his body shrank from it.

He had known even as he talked to Sir Joshua that Jeremy sat behind them like a shadow. They had never mentioned his name, there had been no question as to why the Marquis should suddenly have made up his mind to offer for Lucretia's hand.

They had both been aware of all the things that had been left unsaid. They had both known that the reason for the Marquis's action was not far to seek, and they both accepted it as a sensible, business-like solution to an embarrassing situation.

The Marquis turned his horses into the drive of Merlyncourt. The House was beautiful, the afternoon sun glittering on the windows made them glow like jewels against the grey stone.

"Sir Joshua is right! It is the most beautiful place in the world!" the Marquis thought and told himself it was worth any sacrifice, even that of his freedom.

Yet even as he thought of it he felt a vast disinclination to go through with the marriage.

There was something nauseating at the thought of being tied to a girl he had never even seen, a girl with whom he had no interests in common, and who, however attractive she might be, could never be beautiful enough to take his mother's place.

"I will not do it," the Marquis said almost aloud.

Then he checked the words because he remembered his groom sitting beside him.

There were swans moving majestically across the lake, their heads held high above their arched necks, their white feathers reflected in the silver water.

Their grace and beauty reminded him of the women he had known. The manner in which the Duchess of

Devonshire would enter a room her golden head glittering with a crown-like tiara having a grace that was indescribable.

Georgina Devonshire! And now he had to be content with a dark-haired chit called Lucretia!

Hester! He thought of Hester, and before his eyes came a vision of her perfect body against the blue silk coverlet, naked except for the two strings of black pearls round her neck.

Hester with red hungry lips, her arms stretching towards him, her body moving against his!

The Marquis felt a sudden urgency to be with her, to hold her close to feel their passion rising irresistible and compellingly exotic. A passion which was so overwhelming that it could make him forget everything else.

Hester! He wanted her!

The Marquis drew up his Phaeton at the front door.

"Change the horses," he said to the groom, "I am leaving for London immediately."

He went up the steps and entered the great hall of Merlyncourt.

"I need Hester," he said to himself, "and tonight I need think of nothing else!"

CHAPTER 4

Lucretia heard the carriages arriving.

Her lips felt dry and her heart was beating violently against her breast. This was the moment for which she had waited! It was for this that she had worked until at times she felt she could cry from sheer exhaustion!

Ivor Odrowski was, she discovered, a perfectionist. He could not be satisfied with anything that was not exactly right and he would not tolerate the second-rate.

At times she almost hated him because he drove her on and on to do better even when she felt it was impossible.

Yet all the time she had known it was worthwhile, that only by reaching her goal, by achieving what she had set out to do, had she any chance of captivating the Marquis.

Half way through the three weeks she had allowed Ivor Odrowski for his coaching, she began to see the difference.

Even before her new clothes were finished, she knew that she not only looked different and behaved differently, but she was different in herself.

Ivor Odrowski was creating a character and she began to assume the role, until she was no longer acting, but behaving as she herself had wished to behave.

Her clothes were entrancing! Odrowski produced a young Frenchman who had escaped to England because he had no wish to serve in Napoleon's armies.

He was a sensitive, almost feminine type, which certainly enhanced his creative ability.

The gowns he designed for Lucretia looked lovely

enough when he brought her his sketches. But when they were executed by one of the most expensive dress-makers in Bond Street, they were breath-taking.

Odrowski's teaching extended to everything, to Lucretia's hair, to her hands, to her face.

He taught her how to shade her eyelids so as to make her eyes larger and more seductive. He taught her how a touch at the corners could make them slant a little and become mysterious.

He was far too clever to make Lucretia appear gaudy or over-do the cosmetics.

Instead he managed to throw into prominence the clarity and whiteness of her skin, to draw attention to her eyes, to the perfect curves of her mouth, and sharpen the impact which her winged eyebrows made together with the perfect symmetry of her face.

"You are very beautiful, Mademoiselle," he said once, "but remember that to be really beautiful you must think beauty! To portray beauty the impetus must come from the heart; a surface veneer is never enough."

Lucretia knew that was the truth and because she wanted so desperately to be beautiful for the Marquis, any free time she had when she was in London, she spent in reading books which elevated the mind or in looking at pictures which delighted the eye.

Now she would know whether she had been success-ful or not!

She tried to tell herself that she must remain calm and that any agitation she felt within herself would show on her face.

But it was hard, when she knew that downstairs waiting for her was the man she had admired for five years, the man she had thought about and dreamt of. The man who had become an almost inseparable part of her life.

And yet she had never met him!

With her father Lucretia had chosen the dinner party with great care. It was essential for one thing, Lucretia knew, not to have people who were so familiar with her appearance that they would exclaim at the change.

Sir Joshua had invited a number of intelligent and important men.

While they did not belong to the gay, pleasure-loving circles which surrounded the Prince of Wales, they were all distinguished and in many cases had a unique position in the particular society in which they moved.

There were more men than women, and this Lucretia decided was a wise move. For she was determined that the Marquis should find the evening intellectually stimulating.

As it happened, the Marquis was surprised to find when he entered the Salon one man whose speeches he had read with admiration, and another whose book had been a literary success the year before.

There were other guests whom he recognised as being well worth knowing. One was a great name in the North, another, as Admiral Cornwallis had told him several weeks ago, knew more about the Navy than those who served in it!

Almost subconsciously, the Marquis had expected the dinner party at which he was to meet Lucretia for the first time would be embarrassing.

But now as champagne was offered to the guests by powdered footmen, he found himself responding to talk which even so early in the evening seemed unusually brilliant.

It was after he had been talking for some fifteen minutes that the Marquis realised that Lucretia had not yet appeared.

At that moment the Butler announced in stentorian tones:

"Dinner is served, Sir, and Miss Lucretia begs that you will not wait for her."

"I must apologise for my daughter," Sir Joshua said to his guests, "but she was in fact delayed on her journey from London. I understand there was an accident on the road."

As he spoke he offered his arm to the most important lady present. The other gentlemen guests who had studied the plan of the seating at the Dining-Room table courteously escorted their partners in order of precedence.

The Marquis had already seen that he was to pair with Lucretia, and so with four other gentlemen who were surplus, he waited until Sir Joshua had led the way from the Salon followed by the paired guests.

Chatting to the Colonel of a Calvalry Regiment who was home on leave, the Marquis reached the Hall.

As he did so he heard the Butler exclaim:

"Here comes Miss Lucretia, My Lord."

The Marquis followed the servant's eyes to the top of the stairs.

Two small black boys dressed in turbans and tunics of gold lamé were each holding a huge gold candelabrum lit with six candles.

Between them was a woman!

Very slowly, with a grace and dignity that was unmistakable, she started to descend the wide staircase, the black boys on either side of her.

Lucretia was wearing a dress of pigeon-blood red which threw into prominence the almost dazzling whiteness of her skin.

It was transparent and it was possible to see quite clearly the exquisite outlines of her figure and yet it shimmered and glimmered like tongues of fire with every step she took.

Round her neck was a magnificent necklace of rubies. It had belonged to her mother, but Lady Mary had thought it too spectacular and had seldom worn it.

There were bracelets to match on Lucretia's slim wrists and her hair plaited and piled high on the top of her head in the shape of a crown glittered with the same gems.

She looked completely unlike anything the Marquis had anticipated, yet at the same time exceedingly beautiful and very much older than her age.

He moved automatically towards the bottom of the stairs, and when she reached him without hurrying she sank down in a low curtsey. He was aware that she was looking at him from under her long dark eyelashes as she said in a very soft voice:

"I must apologise, My Lord, for being so tardy in greeting you."

The Marquis bowed, and taking her hand in his raised it perfunctorily to his lips.

"We meet at last, Miss Hedley," he said in his deep voice. "I had begun to think you were a legend and did not really exist!"

"Legends have a habit of being over-romantic or distressingly tragic," Lucretia answered. "I hope that reality will not prove disappointingly ordinary."

"How could you imagine it could be?" the Marquis asked gallantly.

The other gentlemen had gone ahead towards the Dining-room and they moved down the corridor, the small black boys with their lighted candalabra walking on either side.

"Your entourage is certainly spectacular!" the Marquis remarked and Lucretia felt there was a hint of laughter in his voice.

"I am glad you should think so," she replied, "and you, My Lord, are even more handsome than you appear through a telescope."

"Through a telescope!" the Marquis exclaimed in astonishment.

They had reached the Dining-Room and as she was hostess Lucretia sat at one end of the table in a huge chair of emerald green velvet in which she appeared to glitter like a precious jewel.

The Marquis realised that, though Lucretia's appearance might be sensational, everything else in the Dining-Room was unobtrusive and the perfection of good taste.

The table was not over-decorated, there were not too many ornaments each in their way priceless and he anticipated that the food and wine which Sir Joshua would proffer for his guests would be superlative.

He, however, found himself extremely curious, and as soon as everyone was seated he said to Lucretia:

"Will you explain what you meant, Miss Hedley, when you said you had seen me through a telescope?"

"How else could I enjoy the beauties of Merlyncourt and the magnificence of its owner, except from the Look-out?" she answered.

The Marquis frowned for a moment and then he exclaimed:

"Of course! The Look-out on Coombe Hill! I used to go there as a boy!"

"Then you will recall that it offers an excellent panoramic view of Merlyncourt," Lucretia said with a mischievous glance at him from under her eyelashes.

"I must admit," the Marquis replied, "that I have deeply resented the fact that once your father owned Coombe Wood, I could no longer ride there."

"It is very beautiful in the spring," Lucretia smiled.

"I shall look forward to your showing me my old familiar haunts," the Marquis said.

"And there is a great deal for you to show me," Lucretia replied. "It will be thrilling to have the entrée to Merlyncourt after so many years of feeling like a poor little goose-girl locked outside your wrought-iron gates."

The Marquis smiled.

"A very luxurious and elegantly gowned little goose-girl, Miss Hedley."

"I was speaking of my feelings, My Lord!" Lucretia replied reprovingly.

Again the Marquis was aware of a glance from under her eye lashes which was both mischievous and provocative.

"And so you watched me through a telescope," he reflected. "I should have been most embarrassed had I been aware of it!"

"You cannot imagine how much I longed to make your acquaintance," Lucretia said. "Instead I had to be content with imagining situations in which we met by chance."

"What sort of situations?" the Marquis enquired with an amused smile.

"I had at fourteen a very fertile imagination," Lucretia replied. "Sometimes the house was on fire, and you rescued me at the last moment from the burning building before it collapsed!"

"I am glad that did not come true," the Marquis remarked.

He glanced as he spoke round the perfectly proportioned room with its fine pictures and valuable furniture.

"And sometimes I rescued you," Lucretia continued, "from fire and pestilence, but more often from a dragon. But undoubtedly a dragon with a very feline face."

The Marquis laughed.

"I quite see that I should have called formally on your father when I inherited Merlyncourt. As it happens, I have already made him my apologies."

"I am sure you would have found such girlish dramatics extremely tiresome," Lucretia said with a change of tone.

"You sound as if you no longer indulge in such flights of fancy," the Marquis remarked.

"I found instead that if one could not attract Prince Charming, there were still other men in the world," Lucretia answered. "It was for me quite a momentous discovery."

The Marquis looked at her a little uncertainly.

Then before he could ask any more questions, she turned to talk to the gentleman on her other side.

When dinner was over Lucretia took the ladies from the Dining-room. She had already asked Sir Joshua not to hurry the gentlemen, but to linger over the port, making sure that the Marquis found their conversation interesting.

So it was growing quite late before finally the gentlemen entered the Salon.

Several of the ladies who had with their husbands driven a long way for the dinner party, were already thinking it was time for their return home.

Lucretia had decided she would not suggest a game of cards.

She noted that the Marquis, after politely exchanging a few words with one or two of the lady guests, had already returned to conversation with a gentleman at the point they must have left it when they had come from the Dining-room.

Several couples said goodbye, and when there were only a few guests left the Marquis detached himself from the man with whom he was talking and came to Lucretia's side.

"Can I speak to you for a moment alone?" he asked.

"But of course, My Lord."

Lucretia led the way from the Salon and through an Ante-room into a Sitting-room that was essentially her own.

It was redolent with the fragrance of lilies, which were not only arranged in huge bowls on various tables, but were also growing several feet high in large pots on either side of the mantelpiece.

As it was still early in the year and the evenings were chilly, there was a fire, and there were only a few candles in silver sconce's to illuminate the room.

With a quick glance the Marquis realised that here were even finer treasures than anywhere else in the house.

The carved and gilded furniture was of Charles II's period, and angels and hearts rioted in profusion over the richly carved mirrors and the frames of the exceptionably valuable pictures.

"What a lovely room!" the Marquis remarked. "And may I add that it is a perfect setting for you?"

Lucretia had moved towards the chimney-piece. She was looking down into the flames and for a moment she reminded him of someone, though he could not think who it could be.

It was something in her features, the expression on her face, and perhaps the turn of her head! He was not certain. He only knew it lay at the back of his mind.

Then he realised that the flames not only glittered on her gown, but that the soft curves of her slender body were silhouetted against their light.

For a moment the Marquis wondered whether she was aware of it. Then with an effort he said:

"I asked to see you alone, Lucretia—and I hope I may call you that—because I have a present for you."

"A present?" Lucretia asked.

The Marquis drew a velvet-covered box from the long tails of his cut-away evening coat.

He opened it and Lucretia saw a large diamond encircled with smaller diamonds, making a ring which was not only exceedingly beautiful but unique in design.

"It is part of a set," the Marquis explained, "which I hope you will accept on our wedding day. It is in fact the traditional engagement ring of all the Merlyncourt brides."

"It is very lovely!" Lucretia said.

He drew the ring from the box. She put out her left hand and he placed it on her third finger. Then he raised her hand to his lips.

"I am honoured," he said quietly, "that you have consented to be my wife. I will do my best, Lucretia, to make you happy."

Just for a moment Lucretia looked into his eyes and she felt herself quiver at the touch of his hand and the depth of his voice.

Something indefinable seemed to pass between them, something which made it hard to breathe.

Then, finding herself afraid of the intensity of her own feelings, Lucretia forced herself to say lightly:

"Yours, My Lord, is the easier task!"

"What do you mean by that?" the Marquis asked releasing her hand.

"You will attempt to give me happiness," Lucretia answered, "but I shall have the more difficult duty— to prevent Your Lordship from being bored!"

"Bored!" the Marquis exclaimed.

"Surely," Lucretia replied, "Your Lordship is aware that you are known in the County as 'the Bored Marquis'?"

"I had no idea that that was my nickname!" the Marquis protested.

"So you see how hard it will be for me," Lucretia said, "to prevent not only a yawn coming to your lips, but to ensure that other people do not notice it."

She spoke mockingly, and after a moment the Marquis said:

"I have an idea, Lucretia, that you are deliberately

66

provoking me. And I am in fact wondering whether I should kiss or spank you."

Lucretia moved away from him, then looked back over her shoulder.

"I am sorry to inform you, My Lord, that such actions, enjoyable though they may be, are reserved for my intimate friends!"

She paused before she added—and there was no doubt she was being provocative:

"Perhaps when we get to know each other better such ideas might be worth considering!"

The Marquis took a step towards her, but already she had reached the door. She opened it and had re-entered the Salon before he could catch up with her.

She showed her ring to her father and the few guests who were still left.

Amid the cries of admiration, which were not without a note of envy, the Marquis made his farewells.

"May I call on you tomorrow?" he asked Lucretia, in a low voice.

"I hope Your Lordship will not think I am being difficult," Lucretia replied, "but I fear I have to return to London. In fact it is doubtful if we can meet before our wedding-day."

"I shall also be in London the day after next," the Marquis answered, "I hope you will allow me to call on you."

Lucretia deliberately hesitated before she said:

"Your Lordship will appreciate that at a time like . . . this there are many . . . people to whom one has to say . . . goodbye! I find it hard to hurt . . . those of whom one is . . . fond."

There was no mistaking the innuendo in her words and the manner in which she spoke them. The Marquis looked at her sharply.

Then Sir Joshua joined them and there was no further chance of an intimate conversation.

It was only when the last guests had gone that Lucretia, alone with her father, sank down on the hearth-rug and bent her head.

Sir Joshua's eyes were very tender as he watched

her. As she did not speak, he said after a few moments:

"He is all for which you hoped?"

"He is even better looking, more impressive, more overwhelming," Lucretia replied.

She looked up at her father and he knew what she asked of him.

"Unless I am a very bad judge of men," he said slowly, "which you know I am not, he was definitely intrigued! You were certainly not what he expected."

"No, that was obvious," Lucretia answered.

"Nothing is worth having if one obtains it too easily," Sir Joshua said.

"I remember your saying that to me when I was a little girl and I fell off my pony," Lucretia answered. "I told you I wanted to be the best woman rider you had ever seen! And you told me it would take time."

She laughed.

"I have never been able to be patient!"

"That is what you have to be now," Sir Joshua warned her.

"I know," she said, "and it is going to be hard."

She whispered deep in her heart that it was doubly hard, because already she loved the Marquis with an almost frightening intensity!

Sir Joshua was right in thinking that the Marquis had been intrigued.

As he drove back to Merlyncourt he found himself thinking of the provocative sparkle in Lucretia's eyes and the manner in which during the whole evening she had fenced with him in words.

"She is beautiful," he thought and realised that she would grace his table and wear the Merlyncourt jewels in a manner he had not for a moment expected that she would be able to do.

He thought, too, that the Prince of Wales and his particular friends, who were all exceedingly fastidious about women, would undoubtedly admire Lucretia exorbitantly.

Then to his own surprise the Marquis asked himself what sort of wife she would make?

He knew now he had taken it for granted that Lucretia would be a quiet, well behaved girl, who would do as she was told, who would stay at Merlyncourt if he wished to be in London alone, and who would make no demands upon either his time or himself.

As the horses turned in at the gates, he remembered Lucretia's description of herself as a poor little goose-girl!

There was nothing even vaguely to warrant such a description, and the Marquis knew that the vague ideas he had formulated of their future relationship would have no substantiation in fact.

As the horses moved down the drive he found himself going over his conversation with Lucretia.

It had been a duel of wits which he might have enjoyed with any of the sophisticated married women with whom he flirted so expertly. Never had he anticipated it might take place between himself and the girl of eighteen to whom he had reluctantly offered marriage!

The Marquis had the feeling that, contrary to his expectation, he had stepped into a maze to which he did not hold the key and from which he might find it difficult to emerge!

Then he told himself he was being absurd.

Good heavens, if at his age and with his experience he could not make a chit of that age behave in any manner he wished, then there was something very wrong!

He went to sleep thinking of Lucretia, and because he woke several times during the night to find himself still thinking of her, he rang for his valet much earlier than was usual and ordered a horse to be brought round from the stables.

It was a fine morning. There had never been such a calm, warm spring and early summer as in this year, after the threat of invasion.

It was almost as if the elements were jeering at Napoleon who had waited fruitlessly all through the previous summer for the right winds and the right tides to get his flat-bottomed boats out of the French harbours.

There was however, because it was so early in the day, a faint chill on the wind which the Marquis found exhilarating.

His horse was over-fresh and he enjoyed the age-old tussle between man and beast before finally he got it under control.

Then giving the stallion his head the Marquis galloped across the Park and turned towards "The Mile."

This was a long straight strip of grassland on which his father had always exercised his horses. But because it bordered on the land which had been sold to Sir Joshua, the Marquis had deliberately avoided "The Mile" since he inherited Merlyncourt.

It was with a sense of pleasure, as he came on to the grassy mile, that he realised that the wooden fence erected by Sir Joshua to mark the boundary of his property, could soon be removed.

Merlyncourt could return to its original proportions, and the fact that it had even been encroached on by strangers would soon be forgotten.

The Marquis intent on his thoughts was moving comparatively slowly.

Suddenly he heard behind him the sound of galloping hooves and as he turned his head to see who was approaching a horse flashed past. As it did so he recognised the rider!

The Marquis had a brief glimpse of two blue eyes with laughter in them and the curve of a red mouth. Then Lucretia was well ahead and he was in hot pursuit.

He realised two things immediately. First that Lucretia rode amazingly well, secondly that she was mounted on a horse that was the equal if not the superior of his own.

The Marquis was noted for his horsemanship, and the stallion he was riding was only too willing to overhaul anything on four legs.

Nevertheless as they galloped down "The Mile," the

Marquis realised that it was going to be hard to catch Lucretia.

Her riding-habit of emerald green velvet revealed her tiny waist, and from her high hat an encircling gauze veil flew out behind her like a flag of defiance.

Press as he would, the Marquis could not overtake her.

He managed to draw almost level but saw the end of the Mile was in sight and almost instinctively drew in his horse.

As he waited for Lucretia to do likewise, she wheeled suddenly to the right, put her horse at the wooden boundary fence, leapt it and disappeared amongst the trees.

Yet even as she jumped, she looked back at the Marquis and he saw the smile on her lips.

He drew his stallion to a standstill and sat looking at the fence. For a moment he contemplated following her, then decided that already she would be half way back to the Dower House.

"Damn it," he exclaimed to himself, "she is certainly unpredictable!"

It was a sentiment he was to express not once but several times in the following week.

At first the Marquis could not believe that it was really Lucretia's intention not to meet him before their wedding-day.

He imagined she might have many last minute things to attend to besides, as she had told him, saying good-bye to her friends.

He knew that she had intended him to believe that there was a number of beaux and suitors to whom she had to make her farewells. But he had supposed that she was pretending to be elusive just to arouse his curiosity.

But when having called no less than three times at Sir Joshua's house in Curzon Street, only to be told that "Miss Lucretia was not at home," he began to believe that she really intended not to further their acquaintance until the wedding-ring was on her finger.

The Marquis was not a particularly conceited man

although he was naturally well aware of his success with women. Also he could hardly be expected to ignore the fact that he was much sought after in the social world.

There was no host who would not welcome him as a guest, and no woman, although he did not dwell on the knowledge, who would not welcome him as a lover if he so much as glanced in her direction.

Yet this girl to whom he was engaged to be married, this chit of no social consequence, was deliberately avoiding him!

Finally the Marquis had received a letter from Sir Joshua asking if he wished to inspect the wedding-presents before they were sent to Carlton House to be on display during the Wedding Reception.

Thinking naturally that Lucretia would be present, the Marquis had gone to Curzon House, to be blinded by silver ornaments, dazzled by glittering jewels, amused by some preposterously ostentatious gifts, only to find that Lucretia was not there!

"I had hoped that your daughter would do me the honour of meeting me here this afternoon," he said to Sir Joshua.

There was just a touch of ice in his voice, which the older man could not mistake for anything but a rebuke.

"She sent her most abject apologies," Sir Joshua replied, "but you will realise, I am sure, My Lord, there has been so very little time to do all those things which Lucretia informs me are absolutely essential before a marriage can take place!"

"I hoped that Lucretia would wish to meet some of my friends," the Marquis said coldly. "The Duchess of Richmond asked us both to dine tonight—an invitation I understand Lucretia has refused."

"I must beg Your Lordship to excuse my daughter," Sir Joshua replied. "I believe she had a very good reason for not accepting Her Grace's most kind invitation."

"I am sure she had," the Marquis remarked dryly.

As he drove away from Curzon Street he was aware

72

that he had found Lucretia's behaviour extremely exasperating.

In fact when finally he waited at the Chancel steps in St. George's, Hanover Square, for the arrival of his bride, he could hardly credit that he had seen Lucretia only twice in his life and on one of those occasions she had not condescended to speak to him!

The Church was filled to capacity with everyone of any consequence in the *Beau Monde*.

Upstairs in the gallery the tenants and the servants from Merlyncourt, the servants from Merlyn House and from Sir Joshua's residences, were leaning forward in curiosity.

Their faces were red with excitement as they watched the famous personages of whom they had heard or read being shown into the pews by the Marquis's special men friends whom he had invited to be ushers.

The Marquis was well aware that Lady Hester, who was looking beguilingly beautiful, had her blue eyes fixed on him with a wistful expression that proclaimed to all and sundry that she was broken-hearted at the thought of the ceremony which was taking place.

The Duchess of Devonshire on the other hand had given the union her blessing.

"You are wise to marry, Alexis," she had said to the Marquis. "Hester and women like her will involve you in a scandal if you are not careful! A nice sensible country girl will give you a stable background and produce the heir you must have for Merlyncourt."

The Marquis could not help wondering if the Duchess, when she saw Lucretia would consider her a "nice sensible country girl."

Even as he recalled the conversation and avoided meeting Lady Hester's reproachable eyes, there was a signal from the doorway and the organ music swelled into a triumphant burst of sound.

The Marquis turned his face towards the altar to stand deliberately at ease beside his best man.

The music was loud, but his hearing was acute and he was aware of a murmur amongst the guests.

He did not turn his head until Lucretia on the arm

of Sir Joshua had practically reached his side.

Then as he glanced at his wife-to-be he understood why there had been a murmur that had almost been one of applause at her appearance.

After the manner in which she had been dressed on the night of the dinner party at the Dower House, the Marquis had anticipated that she would not be attired conventionally and he had been right.

Lucretia was dressed not in white, but in silver.

It was a silver that glittered and glimmered because it was embroidered with diamanté, and her veil, falling from a huge diamond tiara, was also embroidered with tiny dewdrops which flashed iridescent in the light of the candles.

She carried lilies, but they were not the conventional lilies which had scented her sitting-room, but huge tiger lilies which had only this year been introduced into England. They were tawny gold as the sun against the moonlit silver of her wedding gown.

She held her head high moving as if she were a queen, neither shy nor abashed as was traditionally to be expected of a young bride.

Instead she was all woman, a goddess expecting and commanding the adoration of those who worshipped at her shrine.

Lucretia's eyes met those of the Marquis and he knew again as he looked at her that she was in fact the most unpredictable person he had ever met.

There was something enigmatic about her, something he did not understand.

Then as they moved side by side to stand in front of the Bishop, he could no longer look at her, but only be acutely conscious of her presence.

The service began.

Afterwards Lucretia could never remember the prayers or even the responses. She heard the Marquis's deep voice steady and resolute, and the soft musical tones in which she spoke, almost as if they had nothing to do with her personally.

She felt as if this was a performance, an act, something happening outside herself and in which she had no real part.

They went to the vestry, signed the marriage certificate and walked down the aisle, Lucretia's gloved hand on the Marquis's arm.

She saw a sea of faces but was aware of only one— a woman whose blue eyes blazed hatred, whose beautiful face seemed for a moment contorted as she and the Marquis passed by.

Lucretia had never seen Lady Hester, but the much acclaimed beauty had been described too often for her to be mistaken in identifying her.

Just for a moment she wanted to cry out because Hester Standish was so beautiful, even lovelier than she had known she must be.

Then she and the Marquis were moving through the throng outside the Church and stepping into an open carriage that was to carry them to Carlton House.

There were crowds lining the streets the whole way, waving handkerchiefs, shouting, and wishing them good luck.

It was impossible to do anything but bow and smile in acknowledgement, and there was no question of a private conversation before the horses drew up outside the porticoed door of Carlton House.

The Prince of Wales received them in the Chinese Drawing-room.

"You make a very beautiful bride, my dear," he said to Lucretia. "Merlyn is a lucky man. He did not tell me he had found anyone so lovely, so unique. He must have you painted!"

"I intend to do so," the Marquis answered, "and I shall ask you, Sire, to recommend which artist you think would do her justice."

The Prince was pleased as always when his advice was sought.

"We will have to consider it very carefully," he replied, "but Lawrence does me better than anyone else."

The Prince was very fat, Lucretia thought, but at the same time there was a charm about him that was almost irresistible. And there was no doubt from the expression in his eyes that he was sincere when he said he admired her.

She could feel his finger tickling the palm of her hand as he held it for a long time, until other guests arriving from the Church were announced and Lucretia curtsied and moved away.

"There are so many things I want to see," she said to the Marquis. "Papa will be thrilled! He has so often talked of the wonders of Carlton House."

She had spoken spontaneously without thinking, and now she added:

"I am sure that is not what one should say to one's husband immediately after one's wedding!"

"I do not believe it has ever been recorded what is a correct topic," the Marquis remarked. "Perhaps I should ask you if you are all right, but I can see the answer with my own eyes."

Lucretia smiled up at him.

"And let me be equally generous as this is my special day," she said, "and tell you that I am sure you are without exception the most handsome bridegroom who has ever graced a social gathering of this sort."

"You are speaking from experience, I suppose," the Marquis teased.

"On the contrary," Lucretia replied. "I am basing my assumption on historical fact but where Royalty is concerned, with the exception of our host, it is not much of a compliment!"

The Marquis laughed as she had intended he should, and then they took their place in front of great banks of hot-house flowers to receive the congratulations of the guests.

It was exceedingly hot because the Prince, afraid of draughts, always had his houses suffocatingly over-heated. With the flow of champagne faces soon grew crimson and voices rose as restrictions were loosened.

"Lady Hester Standish."

Lucretia heard the name announced and saw the beauty she had noticed in the aisle of St. George's curtseying to the Prince.

Then Lady Hester was in front of them.

There was no doubt that she was as lovely as an angel! Her blue eyes were misty with unshed tears and her full lips trembled as she took the Marquis's hand in both of hers and said in a faint and tremulous whisper:

"Oh Alexis, my heart bleeds for you!"

Lucretia glanced at the Marquis and saw, as she expected, that he was looking embarrassed. No man likes a scene especially immediately after making his marriage vows.

He did not reply, and Lady Hester ignoring Lucretia completely walked away.

There was a moment's interval before the next guest reached them and the Marquis said quietly:

"I apologise."

Lucretia turned a smiling face towards him.

"Why should you?" she asked. "I can assure you, My Lord, I have suffered far worse this last week! Bleeding hearts are a gorey morsel, which have always given me indigestion."

The Marquis's lips twitched. Then, as if he could not help himself, he laughed.

CHAPTER 5

Although the wedding ceremony had taken place at eleven o'clock and the Prince of Wales sat down to luncheon at noon, it was nearly three before the Marquis and Lucretia could leave Carlton House.

Contrary to what was expected of a bride and groom, they left in the Marquis's Phaeton drawn by four magnificent horses.

The weather was fine and Lucretia felt that she could not bear to spend the long hours to Dover cooped up in a closed carriage.

She had therefore sent a message to the Marquis to say that she was certain he would feel as she did that they would progress faster and certainly find it more pleasureable if they travelled in his Phaeton.

She knew as he drove his horses with an outstanding skill through the traffic and then when they reached the Dover Road, gave them their heads, that he was enjoying the drive as much as she was.

She looked entrancing, and was well aware that her appearance had excited the admiration of the Prince's guests when having changed in one of the bed-rooms at Carlton House she came down the graceful double staircase to find the Marquis waiting for her in the Hall.

Her "going-away" dress and coat were of deep strawberry-pink batiste, embellished with braid and pearl buttons. Her bonnet was tied under her chin with pink satin ribbons.

The heat of Carlton House and the excitement had raised two faint patches of colour in her cheeks, which with the light in her eyes seemed to make her glow with a new radiance.

There was no doubt that the congratulations which the Marquis heard from his friends were given in all sincerity, and enveloped in a cloud of rose petals as they drove away Lucretia could not be mistaken in thinking that the reception had been a great success.

She was well aware that men disliked chattering when they were concentrating on their horses, so she was silent until, when they had left the outskirts of London, the Marquis turned to look at her and said with a mocking note in his voice:

"You were certainly a sensation!"

"I hope it did not embarrass you," Lucretia answered.

"Not in the slightest," he replied. "I always enjoy the unexpected."

"Let us hope that you continue to do so," Lucretia said a trifle enigmatically.

They were moving very swiftly and there was little occasion for conversation. Lucretia also guessed that the Marquis was intent on beating the record to Dover, which was just under four hours.

When they drew up at a Posting Inn in a picturesque village, she realised they had reached the half-way mark.

They had certainly done it in record time, for the Marquis when he looked at his watch found that it was only just after 4:30.

"If we do not linger too long," he said, "we should reach our destination at about half after six."

"You have driven magnificently," Lucretia said with a smile.

She allowed the grooms to assist her down from the Phaeton and walked into the Inn.

The Proprietor's wife in a mob-cap escorted Lucretia up to a bed-room on the first floor.

"I hopes Your Ladyship finds everything you require," she said anxiously. "I'm afraid we weren't able to light a fire."

"I do not need one," Lucretia said.

"The chimney's being repaired, M'Lady," the Inn Keeper's wife continued apologetically. "This room was thick with smoke when ever we'd a fire in the private parlour below. I hopes Your Ladyship will not be chilly."

"No indeed," Lucretia smiled, "all I want to do is to wash."

"If your requires anything else, M'Lady, you've but to ring the bell."

"I will do that," Lucretia said.

The woman curtseyed and withdrew. Lucretia pulling off her bonnet crossed the room to the wash-hand-stand where she saw hot water was waiting for her in a polished brass can.

She was just about to pick up the can to pour the water into the china basin, when she heard the Marquis ejaculate:

"Hester, what the devil are you doing here?"

Lucretia looked round in bewilderment, and then she heard a soft and seductive voice reply:

"I had to see you, Alexis."

For a moment the voices seemed quite uncanny. Then Lucretia remembered that, as the Inn Keeper's wife had explained, the chimney was being repaired.

The bricks from the back of the fireplace had been removed and it was quite obvious that the Marquis was speaking to Lady Hester in the room below.

"How can you do anything so reprehensible?" the Marquis was saying severely. "You should not be here, Hester, as you well know."

"I left the reception early," she said, "I wanted to see you and I knew this was where you would change horses."

"You must go away at once," the Marquis said firmly.

"You deceived me, Alexis, and you have to give me an explanation."

"How have I deceived you?" the Marquis enquired.

"By telling me you were marrying a simple, conformable country girl," Lady Hester answered. "The chit you have just armed down the aisle at St. George's is neither simple, nor I imagine conformable! And she certainly does not look to me like a wench from the country."

"I am not prepared to discuss my wife," the Marquis said loftily.

"Oh, Alexis, how can you be so cruel to me?" Lady Hestern asked passionately. "You know I love you and you promised that, if you married, your wife would stay at Merlyncourt and produce children! How can I be certain that this gawdy serpent will do anything of the sort?"

"I am on my honeymoon, Hester," the Marquis replied, and there was a note of strong irritation in his voice. "You have already embarrassed me once today I cannot contemplate what Lucretia will think if she comes downstairs and finds you here. Go home, Hester, and behave yourself."

"And what shall I do at home but think about you?" Lady Hester asked. "I want you, Alexis, and I know you want me! It would be bad enough to contemplate your spending your honeymoon with any woman, but it is worse that you have chosen a wife who is in every way the opposite of what you promised me she would look like."

"I promised you nothing, Hester," the Marquis said sharply, "and I will not have you upsetting me by behaving as you are now."

There was a little pause and then Lady Hester said softly:

"And how will you stop me? I do not believe that you would wish to cut me entirely out of your life! Anyway I shall refuse to allow you to do so!"

"Go, Hester, go now, immediately!" the Marquis said.

There was no mistaking the authoritative command in his voice.

"Very well, I shall go because you ask me to do so," Lady Hester replied. "But tonight when you hold that creature in your arms you will be thinking of me. You will be remembering the wild passionate moments we have enjoyed together. You will be feeling my mouth— my arms round your neck—my body close to yours!"

Lady Hester's voice was becoming almost inaudible, and Lucretia guessed she had now moved nearer to the Marquis because her voice ended suddenly as if she pressed her lips against his.

There was a long silence and it seemed to Lucretia that the only sound was the beating of her own heart.

Then she heard Lady Hester's voice with a note of triumph in her tone:

"Forget that if you can! Goodbye, Alexis. I shall be waiting for you the night you return to London."

There was the sound of a door closing and Lucretia drew in her breath.

For a moment she felt as if she wanted to scream, to go down stairs to rage at the Marquis and, if she was still in the Inn, at Lady Hester.

Then even as she realised how foolish such an action would be, a cool calmness seemed to bring her not only pride and self-control, but a sense of iron determination to win the Marquis—whatever the odds against her succeeding.

They reached the delightful house which had been lent them by the Earl and Countess of Brora at exactly half after six.

The Marquis was delighted and accepted Lucretia's congratulations, that of his grooms and out-riders who had accompanied them on their journey, with a smile of satisfaction.

He had of course sent his own horses ahead to the Inn, so that the second part of their journey had been even faster than when they had been handicapped by the London traffic.

"You must be tired, M'Lady," the Housekeeper said as she escorted Lucretia upstairs to a magnificent bedroom with a fine view over the Downs.

Far in the distance Lucretia could see the blue of the English Channel.

"No, I am not tired," she answered. "I find it very exhilarating to travel fast."

82

"It's too fast if you ask me, M'Lady," the elderly Housekeeper remarked. "I am always hearing of nasty accidents on the road, and it's not surprising when Your Ladyship remembers that people travel faster than God intended them to do."

Lucretia did not answer and was glad to find that Rose, who had gone ahead with the luggage and the Marquis's valets was waiting for her.

"You made a very beautiful bride, M'Lady," Rose said. "Everybody in the Church was saying they could not imagine it'd be possible to find a more handsome couple than yourself and His Lordship if they searched the whole world."

"That is a delightful thought," Lucretia smiled.

Despite her protestations to the Housekeeper, she was glad to sink into a warm bath that had been prepared for her, and feel the scented water soak away her fatigue and stiffness of sitting so long.

There was always a lot of movement in a Phaeton, and that in itself was somewhat fatiguing, however much one enjoyed the journey.

Rose dressed Lucretia in one of the dramatically beautiful gowns that had been designed for her, and she went down to the Salon.

The house was by no means as imposing as Merlyncourt, nor did it contain any outstanding treasures. But it was decorated in excellent taste, and there was no doubt that the Countess of Brora had arranged everything with the utmost regard for comfort.

The dinner was delicious, and Lucretia and the Marquis sat at the table talking long after the servants had withdrawn.

Lucretia was aware that he was knowledgeable in so many subjects about which she also knew a great deal.

Horses were an easy subject, for her father had always owned some of the best horse flesh that was to be found on any race course.

She had also studied Art since she was very small, and she had read so many books that it was not hard to keep the Marquis interested, amused and, she told herself, secretly intrigued.

She used every artifice that Mr. Odrowski had taught her to make herself appear alluring, but it was her natural wit and an extensive learning which stood her in best stead at this the first meal at which they had been alone.

When finally they reached the Salon, Lucretia looked at the clock on the chimney-piece and said:

"It has been a long day, My Lord. I am sure you will understand if I tell you I am ready to retire."

"Of course," the Marquis answered.

He walked with her to the foot of the staircase, then taking her hand he lifted it to his lips.

"Did I tell you how beautiful you looked today?" he asked.

"I shall be very disappointed if you omit to do so again," she replied.

She smiled at him enticingly as she spoke, then without waiting for him to say any more, walked up the staircase to her room.

It was half an hour later that the Marquis after knocking perfunctorily on the door, opened it and entered.

Lucretia was not, as he had expected, in bed, but was sitting in the window-seat with the curtains drawn back so that the sky silhouetted her head.

The Marquis noticed immediately that she was not wearing a diaphanous or frilly négligée such as he had expected she would do, and which would have seemed in keeping with the other spectacular garments she had worn since he had made her acquaintance.

Instead she was dressed in a white silk wrap with wide sleeves, severely unadorned, not unlike a monk's robe.

Her dark hair fell down her back almost to her waist and her face as she turned it towards him as he entered held a serious expression.

Suddenly the Marquis realised of whom she had reminded him that first night when he had watched her face in the light of the flames in her private sitting-room.

84

She had, he thought, the face of one of the young Madonnas so beloved of the early Italian painters.

He closed the door behind him and advanced slowly across the room, wearing a long brocade robe which glittered faintly in the light of the candles.

"Not in bed, Lucretia?" he asked.

"No," she replied, "I wish to speak to you, My Lord."

"I should have thought it was a little late for conversation," he answered.

There was a hint of laughter in his voice, but as he drew near enough to see the expression in her eyes, he asked perceptively:

"What is the matter?"

"I overheard what was said between you and ... Lady Hester this afternoon," Lucretia replied.

There was a quick frown between the Marquis's eyes.

"Did you listen at the door?"

"The fireplace was being repaired," Lucretia explained. "Your voices carried up quite clearly to the room above."

There was a little pause and then the Marquis began: "I must ..."

"Please do not apologise," Lucretia interposed swiftly. "I am well aware that you did not seek such a meeting and that it was forced upon you. But at the same time, My Lord, let me make it very clear that I have no intention of being a 'simple conformable wife' who produces children at your command."

The Marquis made an impatient gesture and walked across the room to stand with his back against the fireplace.

"This, as you well know, is extremely embarrassing, Lucretia," he replied. "Lady Hester is impulsive and often behaves in an extremely disreputable manner. I am well aware, however, that that is no excuse for what you overheard, and I can only ask you to be generous enough to overlook it and forget that anything unpleasant spoilt our wedding day."

"It is not spoilt as far as I am concerned," Lucretia said. "All I wish to tell you is that I have no intention

85

of playing the part which I now see was obviously expected of me. I am your wife, My Lord, but until it suits me I intend to remain your wife...in name only."

"You might be expected to make such a decision under the circumstances," the Marquis said slowly. "But at the same time it is not a very practical one. We are married, Lucretia, and I hope, as I have told you already, I will be able to make you happy. To live in an unnatural manner would surely not further such an aspiration."

"But I, My Lord," Lucretia replied, "would find it very unnatural to accept the advances of a man who was thinking of another woman."

There was silence. Then the Marquis said:

"I could of course give you my assurance that I should not be doing anything of the sort."

"Could you really expect me to believe you?" Lucretia enquired.

There was a note almost of derision in her voice and the Marquis said sharply:

"Do not let us be over-dramatic about this, Lucretia. I assure you that Lady Hester belongs only to my past. I think you will find that we will deal very well together if you forget what I can only describe as an extremely unfortunate incident."

"I will certainly do my best to forget it," Lucretia answered.

"Then let me show you," the Marquis said, "that being married to me can be exceedingly pleasant."

He moved towards her as he spoke, a confident smile on his lips. Lucretia rose to her feet.

"I am quite certain I shall enjoy being married to you," she said quietly, "but I have never yet, My Lord, allowed a man to make love to me who had not given me his heart."

The Marquis stopped dead in his tracks.

"Are you telling me, Lucretia, that you have already taken a lover?" he asked.

"I am telling you nothing," Lucretia answered, "and I cannot believe that either of us wish to make a confession of what has happened in the past, although undoubtedly such revelations might be amusing, to say the least of it!"

She flashed him a provocative glance as she spoke. Now there was a glint of steel in the Marquis's eyes as he said:

"This all appears to me to be extremely nonsensical and will certainly render our marriage a farce, if nothing worse. You are my wife, Lucretia, and the sooner all these foolish barriers between us are demolished, the better."

He moved once again towards her and now Lucretia said quietly:

"I think not, My Lord."

Suddenly the Marquis was still. Lucretia, taking her hand from behind her back, had revealed that she held a pistol in it.

"Are you crazed?" he enquired.

"I am very sane," Lucretia answered. "For, My Lord, I have no intention of being left disconsolate and with child at Merlyncourt while you enjoy yourself in London."

There was a pause while the Marquis's grey eyes were fixed on Lucretia's. As if she guessed what was on his mind, she said:

"I am a good shot, My Lord. I shall not kill you, but I think you would find that a bullet wound in the arm would prove extremely uncomfortable for the next few weeks."

Quite suddenly the Marquis threw back his head and laughed.

"I surrender!" he exclaimed. "You have certainly been a surprise since we first met, Lucretia, and never more than at this moment! Let me bid you goodnight."

He put out his hand as he spoke and without thinking she laid her fingers in it.

With a sharp movement which made her give a little cry of sheer fear, he pulled her roughly to him and with his other hand took the pistol from hers.

After her first cry she made no effort to struggle, but

stood quite still within his arm, her body close against his.

He looked down into her face.

"This is just to show you, Lucretia," he said, "that you cannot be on guard all the time! Also I have a rooted dislike of having a gun pointed at me—especially by a female."

He slipped the pistol into his pocket. Then he said:

"I have never yet forced myself upon a woman who is unwilling. So let me assure you that you can have your way and my promise as a gentleman that I will not touch you unless you wish me to do so."

He took his arms from her and stepped back.

"Goodnight, Lucretia."

She stood staring at him. Once again took her hand and raised it to his lips.

Then before she could find words in which to say anything, he had left the room closing the door quietly behind him.

Lucretia walked into the breakfast room and she was smiling. The Marquis looked up in surprise, then rose to his feet.

"Good morning, My Lord."

She was wearing a habit of sapphire-blue velvet. There was a sparkle of sapphire and diamonds in the laces at her throat. She was well aware that she looked extremely elegant and that the colour was most becoming.

"You are early, Lucretia!" the Marquis exclaimed. "Most fashionable ladies stay in bed until noon."

"Only when they have been up late the night before," Lucretia answered, "or been unable to sleep."

She sat herself at the table and helped herself from the silver dish profered her by the Butler.

When the servant had left the room, the Marquis said with an amused note in his voice:

"I presume you are telling me that you slept well."

"Indeed, I found the arms of Morpheus most comforting and soporific," Lucretia replied.

"Once again you are attempting to provoke me."

"And why not?" Lucretia enquired, "I have the feeling there is a lamentable lack of entertainment provided for honeymooners."

"And that, I suppose," the Marquis said, "is why you are condescending to accompany me this morning."

"I heard Your Lordship has ordered a horse," Lucretia said, "so I ordered one for myself. Have you any objection to my coming with you?"

"I shall be honoured," he replied.

As she finished her breakfast, Lucretia could not help wondering if the Marquis had lain awake for a long time as she had.

She had found it impossible to sleep while she went over and over again what had happened and asked herself a thousand times if she had done the right thing.

Had she antagonised him completely, she asked or had he found it a challenge to encounter a woman who would not succumb to his much-vaunted charm.

"If he only knew my real feelings!" she thought dismally.

Then she told herself she would go on fighting until she was completely knocked out of the contest.

It was a day of brilliant sun but there was a wind blowing from the sea and it made the horses skittish as they made for the Downs.

Lucretia loved riding at any time, and she told herself there was something fascinating in being accompanied by not only the best looking and most attractive man she had ever seen, but one whom she intended to captivate, however much it might be against his inner inclination.

"Only when he is as much in love with me as I am with him," she told herself, "will I ever be satisfied."

They rode for an hour or more. Then when they should have turned for home, the Marquis suggested they should go a little further still.

"There is a creek about two miles away," he said, "which is supposedly a haunt of smugglers!"

"Then let us look at it by all means," Lucretia agreed. "I do not imagine such ferocious blackguards are likely to be waiting for us at this time of day."

"No indeed," the Marquis answered, "but they may have left a trace of their crimes behind them."

"Why are you interested?" Lucretia asked.

But he did not reply, and it was only after they had inspected the creek and found nothing more ominous than some imprints of footsteps, that the Marquis suggested that they should find something to eat at a local Inn.

"It will not be what you are accustomed to," he told Lucretia, "but I am hungry, as I dare say you are."

"Ravenous!" Lucretia agreed.

Soon they were sitting outside a small thatched Inn, enjoying bread and cheese and drinking home-brewed cider.

"What fun this is!" Lucretia said, putting her elbows on the table and resting her small pointed chin on her hands as she looked up at the Marquis.

"I should have thought you found the food of plough-boys beneath your dignity," he answered.

"You are teasing me," she said. "I assure you I enjoy nearly everything. Except war."

She glanced as she spoke across the Channel.

"What do you know about it?" the Marquis asked with an amused smile.

"I was in Paris the year before last," Lucretia replied.

"You were!" he exclaimed. "Then I am sure like all other English visitors you found the Tuileries magnificent and the appearance of Bonaparte in his plain blue uniform made your heart beat faster."

"Yes, I saw the First Consul," Lucretia said. "Papa and I were taken to the Tuileries and we were of course suitably impressed. There were hundreds of footmen in green and gold uniforms and gorgeously be-gilt peace officers who paraded the Ante-chambers. We were also dazzled by the uniforms of the Aides-de-camp."

She paused and then she went on:

"I was even presented to Napoleon Bonaparte."

"And what did you think of the new Emperor of the French?" the Marquis asked, and there was no mistaking the sneer in his tone.

"I hated him," Lucretia said simply.

The Marquis raised his eyebrows and she went on:

"I have a friend who has become a nun in the Hôpital des petites Soeurs de Jésus. I went to see her."

She gave a sigh.

"The Hospital was filled with soldiers who had been wounded in the war. There were men without legs and arms. Men who had been blinded by the blast of a cannon. Men who were no longer human because their brains had given way under the horrors of what they had endured."

"You should not have seen such things," the Marquis said sharply.

"I worked in the Hospital while I was in Paris," Lucretia answered.

"You did what!" the Marquis ejaculated.

"Not all the time," Lucretia went on, "because that would have annoyed Papa. But from seven o'clock in the morning until noon, I helped my friend and the other nuns who tended the sick. I knew then the truth about Napoleon Bonaparte—he is a monster and a barbarian."

Her voice rang out and after a moment the Marquis said:

"Are you telling me the truth when you say you actually worked in the hospital?"

"Why should I lie?" Lucretia asked.

"But ladies do not do such things!" he protested.

Lucretia smiled.

"You forget I was not of the *Beau Monde* until yesterday when I became your wife. And I believe it is a woman's job to try to alleviate suffering."

"You are a very remarkable young woman, Lucretia," the Marquis said, "and as I have said before, full of surprises."

Just for a moment their eyes met and it seemed to Lucretia that once again something passed between them. Something magnetic which made her quiver.

Because she was shy she rose to her feet.

"Perhaps we should return home."

"I do not wish to tire you," the Marquis said, "because we have been invited to a dinner-party this evening."

"By whom?" Lucretia enquired.

"By the Prime Minister," the Marquis answered. "I found out that he is at Walmer Castle, where you know he lived during his retirement."

"I think it was a great day for England when three weeks ago, Mr. Pitt became Prime Minister again," Lucretia said.

"You must tell him so tonight," the Marquis replied. "And strangely enough, it was the same day May 7th that Napoleon declared himself Emperor of France."

"The fact that Mr. Pitt is back in office is the most ominous warning that the Emperor could be given," Lucretia said.

"Again we agree whole-heartedly," the Marquis replied.

When she was dressing for dinner Lucretia thought with a twinge of apprehension that to meet the Marquis' more serious and distinguished friends was a worse ordeal than encountering the Prince of Wales.

It was not only a pretty face which was important tonight but a clever brain and a sharp wit.

At the same time she asked herself whether if the Marquis had been on his honeymoon with someone he really loved and who attracted him madly, he would have arranged to dine with friends—even the Prime Minister?

Lucretia dressed herself with great care choosing a gown of yellow as clear and brilliant as the spring daffodils and wearing with it a necklace of huge topaz set with diamonds which made her skin fantastically white, yet gave a glint to the stormy blue of her eyes.

When she reached the Salon she dropped the Marquis a curtsey.

"I hope you will not be ashamed of your country bride," she said demurely.

"You might have stepped out of the Arabian Nights!" he answered.

92

But she was not certain if it was a sincere compliment or had a mocking undertone.

Walmer Castle had been built in Norman times and converted by successive Lord Wardens of the Cinque ports and by Mr. Pitt into an extremely desirable residence. It had a fantastic view over the Channel and was, Lucretia thought, very attractive.

But it was difficult to have eyes for anyone but the brilliant Statesman who had been forced out of office and to whom once again the whole nation had turned for help now that war had recommended.

Mr. Pitt had chestnut hair, what the gentlemen called a "port wine" complexion and a pointed nose.

His eyes were bright, his carriage dignified, and he had at first acquaintance, Lucretia decided, a rather grave and detached manner.

But she was well aware that the Prime Minister's eloquence in the House of Commons had a touch of genius, and she was, as she had told the Marquis on the way to Walmer Castle, more thrilled to meet him than any other man in the whole of Great Britain.

There was only a small number of guests to meet them—Admiral the Honourable Sir William Cornwallis, the 60-year-old Commander-in-Chief of the Channel fleet; the General commanding the troops in Dover and a good-looking young naval Commander who was sitting beside Lucretia at dinner.

She was on the Prime Minister's right but she soon realised while he was extremely courteous he was anxious to talk with the Marquis and the Admiral.

She therefore found herself flirting almost outrageously with the handsome Commander, who did not disguise his admiration.

They were half way through dinner when the door opened and the butler announced:

"Major Charles Willoughby, Sir."

For a moment there was an astonished silence, and then as a gentleman entered the room the Prime Minister sprang to his feet with a cry of delight.

"Willoughby, my dear fellow! Where in God's name have you sprung from?"

"From France," the newcomer said and holding out his hand exclaimed, "and the best bit of news I have ever heard, Sir, is that you are in the saddle again."

He looked round the table, saw the Marquis and added:

"Merlyn, the very man I wanted to see! What could be more fortunate?"

"When did you escape?" the Marquis enquired.

"Three weeks ago," Major Willoughby answered. "It has taken me all that time to foot-slog it from Paris. It is not a method of travel I would recommend, I assure you!"

"Nevertheless you achieved it," the Marquis smiled.

"Sit down, Willoughby, and tell us all about it," the Prime Minister interposed. "You know we are consumed by curiosity."

"I have a great deal to tell you, Prime Minister," Major Willoughby said. "That is why I came here as soon as I reached Dover."

"And how did you cross the Channel?" the Admiral asked.

Major Willoughby grinned.

"I expected, Sir, to have to wait for Merlyn or the Navy to rescue me. But a gang of smugglers were most obliging. They landed me early this morning about ten miles down the coast."

"My God is there no stopping them!" the Admiral exclaimed.

"I for one, am very grateful for their services," Major Willoughby joked.

"What is all this about?" Lucretia asked the Commander in bewilderment.

"I expect you remember that when the Armistice ended in May last year," he answered, "the Navy captured two French ships and threw the First Consul, as Napoleon was then, into an insane rage."

"I remember the ships being captured," Lucretia said.

"He at once ordered the arrest of all British travellers in France," the Commander went on, "and some ten thousand civilians were seized. Some, like Sir Ralph

Abercrombie's son, as they embarked at Calais, others as they landed on French soil."

"I recall it now," Lucretia exclaimed. "It was a dreadful act."

"It was indeed," her companion agreed. "Campbell, whom I knew as a boy and who will be the future Duke of Argyll, escaped across the Swiss frontier by disguising himself as a chamber-maid. Thousands of others are still interned, unless like Willoughby they are clever enough to escape."

"It was disgraceful!"

"The internment of civilians is contrary to all civilised precepts," the Commander agreed. "And I think it made us more aware than ever that we are dealing with an un-tamed savage."

"That is exactly what he is," Lucretia cried.

"That is why your husband . . ." the Commander began.

He would have said more but at that moment the Prime Minister rose to his feet.

"As you are the only lady present Lady Merlyn, I am not asking you to withdraw into the Drawing-room alone, but perhaps you will forgive me if I suggest that Commander Naseby entertains you for a short while as I have things of importance to discuss with Major Willoughby and these other gentlemen."

"Yes of course, Prime Minister," Lucretia agreed.

She led the way into the Drawing-room and the Commander followed her.

"I wonder what secrets they are going to discuss," she said curiously.

"It is quite obvious," he answered, "that Major Willoughby has news of other escaped prisoners who can be rescued by the Marquis."

Lucretia looked at him with a question in her eyes and he went on:

"I expect you know, as I was just going to say at dinner, how magnificent he was all last year. He must have brought hundreds of people back from France in his yacht."

"Tell me about it," Lucretia urged. "As you are well

aware, it is very difficult to get him to talk about himself."

The Commander obviously had an almost boyish admiration for the Marquis and he launched into an unbelievable tale.

He told Lucretia the brilliant manner in which the Marquis had slipped into creeks and coves along the French coast and snatched the Englishmen away under the very eyes of the French guards.

"He brought them home despite the fact that a large number of French ships were looking for him! He is as wily as an eel," the Commander finished enthusiastically.

Lucretia, thinking of the Marquis's languid manner which made everyone believe that life for him was one continual boredom, thought this was an aspect of his character she would never have suspected.

She urged the Commander to tell her more. The stories became more and more incredible. The Marquis had appeared in innumerable disguises. He had tricked and bewildered the French soldiers and Napoleon had set a price of twenty thousand gold louis on his head!

It was eleven o'clock but there was still no sign of the Prime Minister and his friends, and Lucretia suggested that they should go out into the garden.

It was dark but the sky was filled with stars. They leant over a wall to look out over the sea.

"Do you think that Napoleon will invade us now?" Lucretia enquired.

"Not a chance!" the Commander answered. "The only possibility of his achieving such a thing would have been last year, but now the British Navy has got what is left of the French fleet bottled up in their ports. We are isolated as an island but we command the seas. That is what is of importance."

"I hope you are right," Lucretia said, "but we are such a very small island compared with the size of France and all the countries that Napoleon has conquered."

"One Englishman is worth six damn foreigners!" the commander declared.

Lucretia laughed.

"As long as we go on believing that we are always sure to win!"

"But of course," he replied.

They talked for a little time of the war, the Commander said as if he could not help himself:

"The Marquis is the luckiest man in the world!"

"Why?" Lucretia asked.

"Because he has won the most beautiful woman it is possible to imagine as his bride!"

"Thank you," Lucretia said demurely.

"I shall dream of you when I am at sea. You cannot prevent me, My Lady, from doing that."

"I would not wish to do so."

"You are everything which a man imagines a woman should be like—face, body and mind," the Commander said hoarsely.

Lucretia drew in her breath. If only the Marquis would speak to her like this!

"Perhaps we should go back," she said softly and added. "Thank you for the kind things you have said to me, I shall remember them."

The Commander took her hand and raised it to his lips. Then she led the way towards the lighted windows. She could see the Marquis looking breathtakingly elegant beside Major Willoughby. They were both laughing and suddenly Lucretia felt piqued.

This should be an important night in her life, but instead the Marquis was absorbed in talking to his friend, perhaps planning a wild and desperate adventure in which she would have no part.

"I will make him aware of me," she thought and with a little cry she fell down.

"What is the matter? What has happened, Lady Merlyn?" the Commander cried.

"I have twisted my ankle," she answered weakly.

He bent down in consternation and she said:

"Perhaps, if it would be no trouble, you would carry me back to the house."

He picked her up in his arms and she knew he was thrilled at the opportunity to do so.

As Lucretia expected, the gentlemen who had by now returned to the Drawing-room stared in astonishment as the Commander resplendent in his naval uniform came in through the French-windows carrying her high against his heart.

She looked very feminine and she hoped pathetic as she explained her predicament.

"It was so stupid of me!" she said apologetically, "but there must have been a hole in the ground."

"I shall speak to my gardener about it tomorrow," the Prime Minister said.

"I think I should take you home," the Marquis said.

"Perhaps the Commander would be kind enough to convey me to my carriage," Lucretia suggested with a flirtatious glance.

"I will carry you," the Marquis said abruptly.

He took her from the Commander and she said good-bye prettily to the Prime Minister, before the Marquis walked with her to the front door.

She felt with a little sigh of satisfaction that his arms were very strong, and yet he set her down gently enough on the carriage seat and pulled the rug over her knees.

They drove off together and the Marquis seemed deep in his own thoughts. After a while he said:

"Do you dislike the sea?"

"No, I enjoy it," Lucretia answered. "I am never sick even during the most violent storms."

"You have been on a sea voyage?" the Marquis asked in surprise. "I thought perhaps you had only crossed the Channel."

"Papa and I went to Greece one year," Lucretia answered. "It was very rough in the Bay of Biscay but I survived."

"I wondered if you would like to see my yacht," the Marquis said. "It is in Dover Harbour and I thought it might amuse you to sail down the coast for a little way."

Lucretia's eyes twinkled. She could guess from the Commander's story of the Marquis intrepid adventures, how a trip in the yacht might end.

But if her husband was not prepared to confide in her, she would not force him to do so.

"I think it is a delightful idea," she said, "and something I would greatly enjoy."

"Good!" the Marquis exclaimed with an obvious air of relief. "We will set out tomorrow morning."

"I shall look forward to it," Lucretia replied.

It was only a short distance to the house where they were staying. Forgetting that she was supposed to have twisted her ankle, Lucretia got out of the carriage without waiting for the Marquis's assistance.

She had walked up the steps and into the Hall before she realised from the expression on his face what she had done.

He said nothing, and with a smile she said:

"I forgot that you might have carried me . . . and I do so love being carried by big strong men."

Just for a moment the Marquis looked stern. Then he stifled whatever rebuke was rising to his lips.

"You are incorrigible," he exclaimed.

Lucretia, walking up the staircase in front of him, had the last word.

"Is that not a much more interesting thing to be than conformable?" she asked.

CHAPTER 6

The weather was warm and fine, but they had a strong Southerly wind which carried them swiftly along the coast.

Lucretia had told the Marquis that she did not wish to take Rose with her.

"Women are always a nuisance on board ship," she said, "and servants are invariably sea sick. I will look after myself."

"Can you really manage?" he asked.

"I can manage very adequately," she replied, "and if I have difficulty with fastening my gowns I dare say you can act lady's maid. You must have had a great deal of practice!"

He was used to her provocative comments by this time and did not answer, but only looked at her with a faint smile in his grey eyes.

"After all," Lucretia went on, "it will only be for a day or so."

She knew as she spoke that the trip would take longer. But the Marquis did not confide in her and she knew that he was deliberately keeping secret his real reason for going to sea.

She thought of how enthusiastic the Commander had been about him, and with what warm sincerity he had spoken of the Marquis's bravery and his brilliant exploits in rescuing so many people from the French.

The Marquis was an extraordinary man, Lucretia thought. No-one could guess from his lazy, bored manner that he had any interest in life other than amusing himself.

And yet she was well aware that men would not speak of him in such terms unless they really had something to admire.

Her father had taught her a great deal about the qualities and attributes which were necessary in a man who was worthy of the name.

Sir Joshua was a shrewd judge, and Lucretia now wondered if he had been deceived, as she had been, into believing that the Marquis was as indolent as he appeared to the world.

"It must be a kind of disguise," she told herself.

As she stood on the deck of the yacht and found they were sailing at a great speed owing to the force of the wind, she thought that this really was an adventure!

She thought too that she was happy as perhaps she had never been happy before! It was a joy which was indescribable to be with the Marquis, and to know that as long as they remained on board he could not escape her company.

The yacht had every luxury. There were four state-rooms, two of them larger than the others and these of course were occupied by the Marquis and Lucretia.

They were side by side and when she went into her own cabin at night, she would think of him divided from her only by a thin wooden partition.

Then her longing for him made her whole body ache and her love seemed to burn within her like a fire which leapt higher and higher every moment they were together.

The Marquis arranged that they should reach harbour each night or anchor in some quiet creek where they could sleep peacefully.

There was however little time for conversation. When they were at sea the Marquis seemed busy on deck, and although they were alone together at meals there were always two stewards in attendance, and the Marquis did not linger after dinner as he had on their honeymoon night.

Instead he usually walked with Lucretia on deck. As they stood looking out to sea she found the twilight and later the darkness very romantic. At the same time there were always sailors moving about or on guard.

They were never actually alone, and though they talked of many things it was hard to be intimate.

Lucretia did not forget Mr. Odrowski's teaching.

"You must never relax," he had told her, "you must never be taken off your guard. You must think yourself into the part until you live it and it becomes not an act but—you."

When Lucretia put on a beautiful gown to dine with the Marquis, she would reiterate the actor's words to herself.

But no acting in the world could prevent her heart leaping when the Marquis appeared, or prevent her at times from feeling very young, very lost and very vulnerable.

"What are you thinking, Lucretia?" the Marquis asked her one night.

They had stayed up on deck so late that the stars had come out in the sky and she had thrown back her head to look up at them.

She did not realise that it gave her white neck a gracefulness which reminded the Marquis of the swans at Merlyncourt.

He had compared them with the Duchess of Devonshire and even with Lady Hester, but he knew now that Lucretia resembled the black swans which he had lately introduced to the lakes and which had seemed to him at the time even more exquisite than their white sisters.

"I was thinking of us," Lucretia answered, dreamily speaking the truth.

"And what were you thinking?" the Marquis enquired.

"I was thinking how insignificant we are," Lucretia answered. "Here under the sky we are only two out of millions of people all over the world striving, struggling, feeling, thinking. And perhaps all our endeavours really mean nothing and are just lost in the sea of life."

"If we really believed that," the Marquis answered, "would we continue to struggle?"

She turned her eyes to look at him.

"That is the right answer," she said almost in surprise.

"I think that just as a human baby and an animal when it is born struggles to live," the Marquis went on, "so we have to struggle to improve ourselves—to develop. And although we are not quite certain what the goal is, we know there is one."

He paused a moment and then he added:

"Perhaps just over the horizon."

Lucretia had never heard him speak in this way before and she said impulsively:

"Of course you are right. Now I no longer feel lonely and afraid."

"You afraid?" he asked. "Of what?"

"I suppose of the unknown future," Lucretia answered. "Life is so over-whelming at times."

"Not if you have faith in yourself," the Marquis answered.

Again she looked at him before she said slowly:

"And that is what you have?"

"I hope so."

"Is it that which makes you so confident, and intimidating to other people."

"Are you frightened of me, Lucretia?"

She felt somehow the question was important. She hesitated a moment and then she said:

"Not physically, if that is what you mean, but in a different way. Perhaps because you are so sure of yourself . . . you make me feel insecure . . ."

"That is something I shall have to change," he said gently.

She looked up at him. In the starlight he seemed very big and powerful.

Yet she had a feeling that if she could be close against him, and if he would only hold her in his arms, she would be afraid of nothing.

Then even as she thought of it, she knew it was too soon. They were still fencing with each other, still fighting a duel of words and perhaps of emotions which neither of them dared name.

"I must be patient," Lucretia told herself in her heart and knew as she had said to her father it was a very hard thing to be.

On the third day Lucretia was well aware that the yacht had altered course. They had stayed at Poole the night before, and now she had no need to look at the compass to realise they were sailing South.

The Marquis had still said nothing to her about going to France, but she was aware that the look-out on the yacht had been doubled and that sailors with telescopes searched the horizon every moment of the day for the sight of a sail.

They were moving into dangerous waters but the Marquis behaved in exactly the same manner as he had when they were running along the south coast of England.

There was nothing in his looks or in anything he said to suggest he had any interest, except a wish to enjoy the sun-shine and the sea breezes.

"It is warm even for June," Lucretia said. "I wonder if the sea is too cold to bathe."

He looked at her in surprise.

"Have you ever bathed in the sea?"

"Very often," she replied. "When we were in Greece before the out-break of war Papa hired a yacht. We sailed round the Greek Islands, picnicked in sandy bays, and we used to bathe in the clear water. It was very lovely. I learnt to swim like a fish."

"I think you would find the Channel extremely chilly," the Marquis warned her, "but sometime we must find a golden shore, where you can show me your aquatic accomplishments."

"I would like that," she said. "I was rather afraid you would be shocked at my appearing in such a state of undress."

"I am very seldom shocked," the Marquis replied.

He noticed that Lucretia smiled and added:

"That is not a challenge, although I am perfectly aware you may use it as another weapon with which to provoke me."

"I will be careful while I am on board, My Lord,"

Lucretia retorted. "You might drop me into the sea and forget about me."

"There is always that possibility," he replied mock-seriously.

She laughed at him. Then said mischievously:

"But of course I could defeat you by swimming ashore and revealing all your secrets to the Emperor of the French."

"Have I any?" the Marquis asked.

"I am sure I could find something about you which Bonaparte would be interested to learn," Lucretia said.

The Marquis's expression did not alter, but she knew instinctively that he was wondering if he should tell her of his plans. Then to her disappointment he decided against it.

They had left Poole very early in the morning and it was growing dusk before on the horizon Lucretia saw a faint shadow which she guessed was the coast of France.

Sir Joshua had insisted that she should be proficient in geography, and she reckoned that the shortest distance to France would bring them to the Cherbourg Peninsula.

If they were to pick up escaped prisoners, it might be a more unexpected place from the French point of view, to stage a rescue than from any of the more obvious bays and creeks facing the Straits of Dover.

As if the Marquis did not wish Lucretia to realise exactly where they were, he made an excuse to draw her down into the cabin before it was possible to see the coastline clearly.

They had dinner and the Marquis remarked casually:

"There is rather a chill wind, I think it best not to go on deck tonight."

"Shall I challenge you to a game of backgammon?" Lucretia asked.

"That will be most enjoyable," he replied. "Excuse me for a moment while I speak to the Captain."

He left the cabin and obviously intended to go up on deck. But the Captain must have come down to see him, for Lucretia heard their voices in the passageway.

She sprang to her feet, crossed the cabin and stood with her ear against the door.

"We should be able to anchor off St. Pierre d'Eglise, M'Lord, in about thirty minutes time," the Captain reported.

"Better keep well in the shadow of the cliffs," the Marquis replied. "We should not be seen in the twilight. And have a boat ready to take me ashore as soon as the anchor is down."

"Very good, M'Lord. Is it two gentlemen you are expecting."

"Lord Beaumont and his son. They will be waiting for me in a place arranged. I will bring them to the boat. If anything goes wrong, Captain, carry out the same orders as I have given you in the past."

"Very good, M'Lord."

The Captain hesitated for a moment and then he said:

"Excuse me, M'Lord, but have you told Her Ladyship?"

"There is no reason for her to know anything about this," the Marquis replied. "However, if I do not return, do not alarm her. Merely say it is a change of rendez-vous and that I shall be perfectly safe."

"As you have been before, M'Lord."

The Marquis gave a little laugh.

"As I have been before. Although there have been narrow squeaks, as you well know."

"Only too well, M'Lord. I must say I am never really at ease until I have you back on board again."

"Thank you, Captain," the Marquis said. "By this time I ought to be able to look after myself. The only real question is, will Lord Beaumont and his son be waiting for us as arranged?"

"We can only hope so, M'Lord."

"Major Willoughby told me they were well disguised, and Lord Beaumont can speak French."

"If they are not there, M'Lord," the Captain suggested, "it would not be wise to hang about for too long."

"No, of course not," the Marquis agreed. "At the

106

same time the Prime Minister is very anxious they should reach England quickly and in safety."

The Captain sighed.

"Then we can only do our best, M'Lord."

Lucretia realised the conversation was at an end and moving swiftly back across the cabin, she was seated at the backgammon board arranging the pieces when the Marquis joined her.

She beat him at two games, realised he was not really concentrating and rose to her feet with a little yawn.

"I think I will retire, My Lord."

"That is a good idea," he said in relief.

She dropped him a curtsey.

"Goodnight and thank you for a very pleasant day."

"A very pleasant day," the Marquis echoed and raised her hand to his lips.

Lucretia walked slowly into her cabin, but once there she started feverishly to take off her evening-gown and put on a dark dress which she covered with a dark cloak.

Then she went to the door and listening realised that the Marquis was in his own cabin, doubtless also changing his clothes.

She slipped up the companionway and onto the deck. The anchor was being let down and a boat was being put over the side.

She waited until it was in the water and then, to the surprise of the men manning it and the young Petty Officer in charge, climbed down a rope ladder and was helped into the boat.

"Are you coming with us, M'Lady?" the Petty Officer asked uncertainly.

"Only as far as the shore," Lucretia replied. "I have a headache and feel a change of scene would do it good. Do not mention my presence to His Lordship until we are well away from the yacht. He might be foolishly afraid there was some danger attached to my short voyage!"

She smiled at the Petty Officer as she spoke and bemused by her condescension he answered:

"I will not mention it, M'Lady."

The boat was in the shadow of the yacht. There were cliffs about a hundred yards ahead of them, but Lucretia could also see a creek and she guessed it was there the boat would land.

The sailors were at their oars and the Petty Officer had his hand on the rudder when Lucretia saw the Marquis appear on the deck above.

There was no-one with him and taking hold of the rope ladder he climbed rapidly down it and stepped into the boat. As he did so, the Petty Officer gave a command and the men started to row towards the shore.

Then as he Marquis sat down in the stern he found Lucretia beside him.

For a moment he did not speak but looked at her in astonishment. She realised that he had not at first seen her because her cloak was black and the hood pulled over her hair had kept her face in darkness.

"Lucretia!" he exclaimed at length in a low voice, "what are you doing here?"

"I am coming with you as far as the shore," Lucretia answered. "My headache grew worse and I needed the air."

"You did not think of asking me if you could do so?"

"Why should I?" she enquired in an innocent voice. "Is there anything wrong in your going ashore?"

"Who said I was going ashore?" the Marquis asked.

"Is is surely very obvious!"

She could feel he was worried and more than a little perturbed at her appearance. So she said:

"I quite understand you wanted to take a walk after so many days at sea. A yacht is very confined."

"Yes, that is what I found," the Marquis agreed in a tone of relief. "It is a wild uninhabited part of the country and I am not likely to be seen."

"No of course not, not at this time of night," Lucretia answered.

They reached the shore and the Marquis said sternly.

108

"You will go straight back to the yacht, Lucretia. Is that understood?"

"But of course," she answered, "although I suppose the boat will be coming back for you. How long do you intend to take on your walk?"

"Only about thirty minutes or so," the Marquis replied.

"Then enjoy yourself, My Lord," Lucretia said. "I expect I shall be awake when you return."

"I expect so," the Marquis replied absently.

Two sailors had sprung overboard and were pulling the boat up onto the shingle.

The Marquis stepped out and without speaking was lost in the shadows of the rock.

The seamen, who obviously had their orders, were pushing the boat back into the water when Lucretia said to the Petty Officer:

"Wait a moment."

"We have to return to the ship, M'Lady."

"Yes I know—but wait."

She made a great play of looking inside her cloak. Then she said:

"The Marquis must have forgotten. He asked me to keep this compass for him and I most regrettably forgot to return it. It is of the utmost importance, I must take it to him."

"But, M'Lady!" the Petty Officer protested.

"It is essential for His Lordship," Lucretia insisted. She turned to one of the sailors holding the boat.

"Would you be obliging enough to lift me ashore? I would not wish to get my feet wet."

"Let me take it, M'Lady," the Petty Officer pleaded.

"No! No!" Lucretia said, "His Lordship would not wish that. He told me explicitly no-one must touch this compass except myself."

She turned towards the seaman as she spoke who was not loth to lift anything so attractive in his arms.

He picked her up and carried her through a few feet of water to the shore.

"Go back at once as His Lordship told you to do,"

Lucretia said to the Petty Officer. "I will return with him later."

"But, M'Lady . . ." the Petty Officer expostulated, only to find that Lucretia had run into the shadows and disappeared.

The Petty Officer was too young and inexperienced to know how to cope with such a situation and decided that the only sensible thing he could do was to obey orders.

Lucretia found a path up the cliffs which were not very high and almost immediately sloped downwards to where there was a rough cart-track running east along a rocky shore.

She felt this would be the direction that the Marquis had taken and by running swiftly she soon had a sight of his tall, broad-shouldered figure hurrying ahead.

She saw that he had now discarded his cloak and was wearing a dark suit which gave him somehow a strange appearance.

The track widened into a roadway, narrow and dusty, leading to a village. Lucretia could see a spire a little way ahead and guessed it was St. Pierre d'Eglise.

The Marquis was only walking, but she found she had to run to keep up with him.

They had almost reached the village and Lucretia could see houses as well as the church ahead. There was a bend in the road ahead, and hurrying round the corner she could not for a moment see the tall figure she had been following.

And then quite suddenly the Marquis stepped out of a hedge to clutch her by the arm.

"Why are you following me?" he asked in French.

Then as she gave a little cry of surprise he exclaimed incredulously:

"Lucretia! What in God's name do you mean by coming after me?"

She looked at him and could see quite clearly in the twilight that his eyebrows were meeting across his forehead and that he was excessively annoyed.

"I thought I . . . might be able to . . . help you," she said weakly.

110

"Help me? In what way?"

"I speak extremely good French."

"You are to go back at once," the Marquis said sharply, "I did not tell you, Lucretia, but I am on an errand of mercy and it could be dangerous."

"I know," Lucretia replied. "You are picking up Lord Beaumont and his son who have escaped from internment."

"How do you know that?"

"I listened," she said simply. "But Major Naseby told me you rescued many people last year."

"Naseby should keep his mouth shut!" the Marquis said disagreeably. "You are to go back. Do you hear me? Immediately!"

"The boat has returned to the yacht."

The Marquis stood irresolute and Lucretia knew that he that he was debating whether he should take her back or continue towards his meeting-place.

"I will be no trouble," she said in a soft voice.

"You are a trouble!" he said crossly. "You have been a trouble ever since I have known you!"

"You had much better accept the inevitable and let me come with you."

"Very well!" the Marquis said as if he had suddenly made up his mind. "We can only hope that everything goes smoothly. If it does not and you find yourself languishing in a French prison, do not blame me."

He did not wait to hear her answer but started to walk down the road. She moved beside him, very conscious of his anger and at the same time content that she should be at his side.

She knew that she could not have waited in the yacht, wondering what was happening to him, terrified lest he should be in danger.

It was one thing to hear of brave deeds, she thought, but quite another to be concerned with those who performed them.

She loved the Marquis—loved him with an intensity which seemed to grow day by day, hour by hour. And she was not so naive as not to realise that what he was doing was in fact extremely dangerous.

Napoleon had a fanatical hatred of the English. It had been a feather in his cap to hold in captivity anyone so distinguished as Lord Beaumont. The news that he had escaped would have alerted all the soldiers guarding the North Coast of France.

It would be obvious that His Lordship would try to return to England. There would be thousands of troops looking for any men who would answer the description of Lord Beaumont and his son, however skillfully they might be disguised.

They had almost reached the village before the Marquis slowed his steps, and standing in the shade of a tree took stock of his surroundings.

The place was little more than a hamlet. There were a few fishermen's houses clustering round a small grey stone church and an Inn, but little else of interest.

"Where are you meeting them?" Lucretia whispered.

"In the church-yard," the Marquis replied, and she knew by his tone of voice, low though it was, that he was still extremely incensed with her.

Moving quietly and keeping in the shadow of the houses, they moved down the village street, seeing no-one about.

They reached the churchyard and Lucretia saw that it was in a bad state of disrepair.

The grave-stones must have been broken and desecrated during the Revolution. There was no glass in the church windows. The weather-vane had been broken on the tower and was hanging at a drunken angle.

The walls surrounding the churchyard were crumbling and the lych-gate, broken off its hinges, was lying on the ground as if someone had thrown it off.

The Marquis walked in followed by Lucretia. There were many large square grave-stones still standing, and Lucretia wondered if the two gentlemen they sought were hiding behind them, or perhaps even in the Church.

As she thought of it she saw that the door of the Church was boarded up. It was obvious that no-one in St. Pierre d'Eglise was able to worship there.

112

It was then as the Marquis stood looking about them that they heard the sound of marching feet.

There were soldiers approaching.

The Marquis looked round quickly, but there was nowhere to hide. Then just as the soldiers came round the side of the Church, he turned quickly to Lucretia and put his arms round her.

"Push back your hood," he said in a voice which only she could hear. "We are a courting couple and perhaps they will ignore us."

He held her close against him and put his cheek against hers. Lucretia knew by the rigidity of his body that he was anxious and apprehensive at the appearance of the soldiers.

But neither of them looked round until they heard the word of command and knew that the squad had come to a halt beside them.

"Here you, what are you doing here?" a man asked in French, speaking in a rough, loud and uncultured voice.

Lucretia and the Marquis turned round to face him and it was not surprising to find he was a Sergeant.

There were four soldiers besides the man who had spoken to them, and the Marquis replied politely:

"I'm meeting my girl-friend, Monsieur."

The Sergeant came nearer and looked up into the Marquis's face.

"What's your name and where do you come from?"

"My name, *Monsieur*, is Pierre Bouvais. I'm a clerk working in Cherbourg. I've come out here, as I told you, to meet this Ma'mselle."

The Sergeant looked at him suspiciously.

"Why did you come all this way?" he enquired.

"Because we have been forbidden to meet," Lucretia interposed, deliberately making her French sound countryfied as she had noticed the Marquis had done.

She did not expect him to speak so well, and she realised that in some subtle way he had appeared to become the clerk he said he was.

There was something nervous and anxious about him as if he were afraid of the soldiers.

"*Voyons, voyons,* you will have to explain this to the officer," the Sergeant said.

"The Officer!" Lucretia exclaimed.

"Anyone found in the churchyard or thereabouts is to be taken for questioning," the Sergeant said in the voice of one who repeats his orders but has no particular interest in them. "Come along now, I haven't time to stay arguing."

"But we always meet here," the Marquis said raising his voice as if in protest. "We come either to the church-yard or else to St. Pierre's Bay at least once or twice a week. What harm is there in that?"

"The Officer will tell you if there's any harm in it," the Sergeant said roughly. "Come along now, I cannot stand here all night."

The two soldiers took the Marquis by the arm while the other two marched each side of Lucretia, and they set off along the road to the village.

As they left the church-yard the Marquis said again:

"I cannot see there is anything wrong about meeting in the churchyard or St. Pierre's Bay. If they are out-of-bounds, someone should have told us."

He spoke in resentful tones and Lucretia realised with a flash of intuition he had twice mentioned St. Pierre's Bay.

That must have been where they landed, and that was where Lord Beaumont, if he was anywhere within hearing distance, would know that he would find a rescue boat waiting to convey him and his son to the yacht.

The difficulty now, Lucretia thought, would be to extract themselves from this difficult situation.

She wondered if Lord Beaumont had already been captured and been forced into saying where he would be contacted by someone from England.

Then she thought it was far more likely that the French were more alert than the English gave them credit for, and were therefore questioning anyone who aroused suspicion all along the length of the coast.

They were marching quickly and she found it difficult to keep up except by almost running.

She was therefore breathless by the time they had covered nearly half a mile and come to the farmhouse.

It was obvious from the number of soldiers standing about in the farm-yard and outside the door of the farm, that it had been commandeered by the military.

Following the Sergeant they entered the house. In a narrow low ceilinged hall he knocked on the door and when there was no answer, entered.

They were in what was obviously a small front room of the farm. The desk had been improvised out of a heavy oak table and was littered with papers, an ink-pot and several quill pens.

The Sergeant crossed the room and knocked on another door on the other side. A voice replied *"Entrez"* and he did so closing the door behind him.

Lucretia looked at the Marquis. In the light of the two lanterns which illuminated the room she realised why he had seemed different even in the distance.

He was wearing a tightly buttoned plain black coat such as a respectable clerk would have as his best. His buckled shoes had heavy soles and his stockings were of thick wool.

He had brushed his hair in a different way, and now as he waited for the return of the Sergeant he drew from his pocket a pair of steel-rimmed spectacles and put them on his nose.

If she had not realised the danger they were in, Lucretia would have laughed.

The Marquis's disguise was brilliant, and she knew that Mr. Odrowski would have approved the manner in which he changed his whole personality. It was not only his clothes, but also how he stood.

He had a nervous flicker of his eyes, and the strangely disfiguring glasses seemed to distort his straight aristocratic nose.

A door at the far end of the room opened and the Sergeant returned, preceded by an Officer.

He was a young man of about twenty-five, a petit bourgeois and Lucretia saw that he was bored with the whole procedure.

"Who are you?" he asked in an aggressive manner,

"and what are you doing in the church-yard at this time of night?"

"I had no idea, *Monsieur*," the Marquis said humbly. "There was anything wrong in meeting my fiancée there. We have often done so before and there has been no trouble."

"And you, where do you come from?" the Officer enquired of Lucretia.

His voice was rough as he began the sentence and softened perceptibly towards the end.

In the light of the lanterns she looked very lovely.

With an effort she swept aside the feeling of fear that was sweeping over her and giving him a glance from under her eye lashes as she said:

"*Tiens, Monsieur*, I come from Paris. But I am staying in the vicinity and monstrous dull I find it. So I have a bit of fun by meeting the gentleman you see here. And if there was anyone more attractive I would be meeting him too."

She gave the Frenchman a glance he could not misunderstand.

"You interest me, *Mademoiselle*," he said and there was a glint in his eye that had not been there before. "Suppose you come and tell me exactly what you were doing in the church-yard tonight. I am sure I should find it very informative."

"I am sure you would, *Monsieur*," Lucretia answered, "and perhaps you could tell me what is happening in the outside world. I might as well be incarcerated in a convent as in this dull place!"

The Frenchman laughed.

"We shall have to see if we can make it more amusing for you," he said. "Come into the other room. I am finishing my supper, I don't want it to get cold."

"No, of course not," Lucretia answered. "I will willingly come with you, *Monsieur*."

She gave the Marquis a glance as she followed the Frenchman to the door and knew by the manner in which he glared at her that he was not only angry at what she was doing, but extremely apprehensive.

"Poor Pierre, he is jealous!" she said to the Frenchman.

"What do you want me to do, *Monsieur*," the Sergeant interrupted.

"Find the Englishman and his son!" the Officer snapped. "Leave one soldier here to guard this man. Better tie him to the chair so he cannot escape, not that he looks as if he wishes to do so."

"I doubt if he'll go without his *chere amie*," the Sergeant smiled.

"Anyway, tie him up," the Officer ordered, "and get back on duty. Those English swine must be somewhere in the neighbourhood."

"I'll find them, Monsieur," the Sergeant said. "Don't you worry."

"You'll have to find them before Major le Cloud arrives," the Officer said, "and don't you forget it!"

He followed Lucretia into the other room as he spoke. She had been listening but also looking round her as she took off her cloak.

This room was larger than the one that had been used as an office. It was better furnished, in the centre was a table on which were the remains of an evening meal.

As the Officer seated himself, an elderly woman, her face lined and weather beaten and resentful, came in from another door and set a pot of coffee down on the table.

Lucretia guessed she was the farmer's wife and was not pleased at having her farm commandeered by the military.

"Another cup," the Officer said sharply.

The woman did not answer but went from the room to return a few moments later to slap a cup and saucer down on the table.

"Sit down *Mademoiselle*," the Officer said, "and let me pour you a cup of coffee. Or what about a glass of wine?"

"I am certain, *Monsieur,* I should enjoy one with you," Lucretia said looking at him flirtatiously.

117

He poured some red wine into an empty glass which stood on the table and filled up his own.

Lucretia noticed as he did so that he emptied the bottle.

"Tell me about yourself," the Frenchman begged.

"There is very little to tell," Lucretia answered, "I am just bored. I assure you, *Monsieur,* I haven't seen anyone as young and as handsome as you ever since I came to this deadly place."

"Then why are you here?" the Officer asked.

"My father is concerned with building ships for the Emperor."

"That accounts for it," the Frenchman said. "But even creatures as lovely as yourself have to suffer in war-time."

"My sufferings are endless, Monsieur, I assure you, but not at the moment."

She sipped the wine.

"May I drink to your success?" she suggested. "I am quite certain that you will be a General long before we have peace."

"There would be peace tomorrow if it wasn't for those cursed English," the Frenchman said.

"C'est vrai," Lucretia agreed with a smile, "but surely the imbeciles must realise they are beaten?"

The Frenchman shrugged his shoulders.

"Who knows what they think?" he said. "Instead let me tell you what I think about you. *Vous êtes très jolie, Mademoiselle.* We must contrive to make your visit far more interesting than it is at the moment."

"How will you do that?" Lucretia asked fluttering her eyelashes.

"Do you really want me to tell you?" he asked putting his face near to hers.

"But what about poor Pierre?" Lucretia enquired. "You cannot keep him here! He will lose his position! His employer is most insistent that he must be at work at seven o'clock in the morning."

Her brain was racing feverishly as she spoke. The French Officer was a slim man who did not look at all muscular.

"Why is he not in the Army?" the Frenchman enquired. "He is a big chap. Just the sort of man we are looking for."

"His eyes," Lucretia said in a sad voice. "He could not hit the enemy at ten yards, he is so near-sighted."

"Oh well, you would think they would find something better for him to do when we are so desperately short of men."

Then as if the subject was of no interest, he said: "Let us go on talking about you, *Mademoiselle*."

"Then why not let Pierre go?" Lucretia enquired. "I really feel nervous in case he is listening to what we say."

"He can't hear through these thick walls," the Officer replied, "and I can't release him until Major le Cloud arrives. Anyone who is suspected has to be properly interrogated by the Major and perhaps appear before the tribunal in Paris."

"*Mon Dieu!*" Lucretia exclaimed, "I had no idea we were so important!"

"You are very important, *Mademoiselle,* that I can assure you," the Officer answered.

He finished his glass of wine as he spoke and put out his hand towards Lucretia. As his fingers touched the softness of her neck, she rose to her feet, smiling beguilingly. An idea had begun to formulate in her mind.

"I will get you some more wine, *Monsieur*."

"No, do not move!"

"I will wait on you. It is a pleasure . . . I assure you."

She had seen another bottle on a side-table and before he could prevent her she had moved behind him to pick it up. As she left the table she took a coffee spoon from the saucer of her cup. She picked up the bottle by the neck.

"We must drink a toast together, *Monsieur*," she said in a seductive voice. "I have been wondering what it should be, and now I know."

"Tell me," the Frechman asked looking round at her. Once again he was seeking to touch her. As his arm encircled her waist she dropped the teaspoon she held in her left hand.

Instinctively he bent down to pick it up and as he did so she brought the bottle of wine that she held in her other hand crashing down on the back of his head.

He fell forward with the first blow and she hit him again. Then as he collapsed onto the floor, slipping from his chair to lie sprawled under the table she picked up her own glass of wine and went to the door still carrying the bottle in her hand.

It was difficult to open the door so that there was only just room for her to squeeze through it, but she managed it.

As she expected, the Marquis was sitting on a chair against the wall, his hands tied behind him. The soldier who had been left in charge was seated by the other door, his musket in his hand.

Lucretia walked towards him and was thankful that he made no effort to rise.

"Your Officer has asked me to bring you a glass of wine," she said ingratiatingly. "He realized that we have a long wait until Major Le Cloud arrives."

The soldier looked astonished. Then with a smile which showed a mouthful of blackened and broken teeth, put out his left hand for the glass.

As he was about to take it from Lucretia, she let it slip between her fingers. It fell to the ground with a crash and smashed into a thousand pieces.

The soldier bent forward in dismay and she brought the bottle of wine down on the back of his head with all her strength.

The first blow was not enough because the force of it was mitigated by his soldier's cap. But a second and third left him sprawled senseless on the floor.

"Good girl!" she heard the Marquis say softly. "Untie me."

She put down the bottle and ran to his side. The knots were tight and for one frantic moment she thought she could not get them undone.

But as she loosened them, the Marquis pulled his hands free and pulled off the rope and with a swiftness

120

she had not thought possible he sprang across the room and blew out the two lanterns.

Then he opened the small casement and cautiously put his head outside.

He did not speak but picked Lucretia up in his arms and pushing her through the window dropped her down on the ground below. Then he clambered after her.

There appeared to be no-one about, but the Marquis was taking no chances.

Keeping close against the walls they crept round the side of the house until they were opposite a large barn as could be found on nearly every farm in France.

The Marquis paused, looked round, then taking Lucretia by the arm pulled her across the open yard at a speed which left her breathless.

She felt they should be going further but dared not speak to the Marquis. It was dark in the barn, but after a moment she could see just dimly two ladders propped on either side leading to the lofts above the stalls which contained the animals.

The Marquis climbed a few steps up one ladder, came down and tried the other.

"This one," he said in a voice little above a breath.

Lucretia went ahead and he followed her.

She could barely stand up in the loft and the Marquis was almost bent double. He pulled the ladder up after him, but now she saw with a sense of dismay there was practically no hay in this loft while she could see that across the barn the other loft was stacked with hay.

"Should we not be the other side?" she whispered.

"No!" he answered sharply. "Go and lie down against the eaves."

She did as she was told and he started to scrape together what remained of the hay until finally there was a small pile just enough to cover her.

It was then, as he was still working, that she heard the sound of voices.

"They are coming," she said with a sudden terror.

The Marquis slowly and without hurrying lowered himself down on the floor until he lay beside her. Then he pulled the pitiful amount of hay that he had collected over them both.

Lucretia felt it would barely cover them! But she was conscious that the Marquis was lying almost on top of her and, frightened though she was, she felt a throb of excitement because he was so close.

Down below there was the noise of soldiers entering the barn.

"They can't be far you fools, you idiots!" a man was shouting. "Why didn't you see them escape?"

"What about them lofts, Corporal?" another man asked.

"Get up that ladder and see what's up there," the Corporal ordered who was obviously in charge.

Lucretia could hear the sound of a soldier climbing up the rickety ladder.

"There's a lot of hay," he said from the top.

"Don't waste time! Dig your bayonet into it, don't miss anywhere a man could hide," the Corporal commanded.

Lucretia knew now why the Marquis had chosen the loft with no hay. She could hear the man jabbing about on the other side of the barn and with a shudder she felt how terrifying it would have been to wait for a bayonet to be thrust into her body or to know that it had pierced the Marquis.

"There be no-one here," the soldier shouted.

"*Allons!*" the Corporal retorted. "Don't waste time. They must have made for the shore. They be English, I'll be my last franc on it."

There was the tramp of men's feet leaving the barn and then as the light of the lantern went away with them, Lucretia opened her lips to speak. But before the words could come to her mouth the Marquis turned and kissed her.

For a moment she was so astonished that she seemed to stop breathing.

Then as a sudden ecstasy like quick-silver ran through her, as she felt the hard pressure of his mouth on hers evoke a rapture she had never known in her whole life, she heard someone cough.

122

She was suddenly rigid. There was a man below. A man who now moved his feet, then turned and walked out into the yard.

Lucretia knew then that she had nearly been caught by the oldest trick in the world. All the soldiers had left except one and he had remained just to see if after all there was someone hiding in the barn who might think, as she had thought he was safe.

Then the Marquis raised his head and her lips were free.

She knew then he had kissed her only to prevent her from speaking, not because, as she had thought for one incredible, wonderful moment, he wished to do so.

CHAPTER 7

Without speaking the Marquis rose to his feet and helped Lucretia to hers. Then he released her hand and picking up the ladder let it down onto the floor below.

Still not speaking he climbed down it and waited for Lucretia to follow him.

The barn was very quiet save for the slow movements of the animals in the stalls.

But there were not many of them and Lucretia found herself thinking that this farmer whose house had been taken over by the military must be a poor man.

It was strange, she was to think later, how in moments of danger one's mind surprisingly flickered away to notice irrelevant and unimportant matters as if it was somehow detached from the immediate crisis.

Drawing Lucretia by the hand, the Marquis moved swiftly across the barn to the big doors.

They had been left ajar by the soldiers, and looking out they could see the lighted windows of the farm and the glow they shed into the yard outside.

It had grown perceptibly darker since Lucretia and the Marquis had been in the barn. Now it was easier than it had been before to slip through the doors and keeping to the shadows of the buildings move from the farm and out into the field.

The Marquis was walking, Lucretia noticed, due South. She thought he must be doing this because the soldiers had gone towards the shore and she guessed that to avoid recapture they must make a wide detour of the area which the Military were investigating.

124

As soon as they were clear of the farm itself, the Marquis started to run.

They were moving over grassland and Lucretia would have found it easy to keep up with him had she not been hampered by the fashionable tightness of her gown.

After she had struggled to hold it up, she stopped and said in a whisper.

"Have you a knife? Can you slit up my skirt. It is almost impossible for me to run in it."

They were the first words which had passed her lips since the Marquis had kissed her to prevent her speaking. And as she saw him dimly in the gathering dusk, she felt again the sudden thrill that had passed through her at the touch of his mouth.

But she knew despairingly that he was not interested in her personally, she was at the moment merely a trouble and a hindrance to their escape.

Without speaking the Marquis drew a knife from his pocket and bending down cut her dress at the back from the knee to the hem. Then he stood up putting the knife back into his pocket.

"We must get away as fast as possible," he said.

"Yes, I know," she answered.

They started to run again climbing down a deep ditch at the end of the field and then moving across another which had been ploughed and sown with young wheat.

This was heavy going, but fortunately there was a copse at one side of it and the Marquis made for the shadow of the trees.

They must have travelled for nearly a mile, and Lucretia's heart was pounding and she was beginning to find it hard to breathe, when at last the Marquis stopped and looked back. He could see nothing, for the darkness had closed in and it was a cloudy night.

"Do you think they will follow us?" Lucretia asked as he did not speak.

"They know eventually we will make for the sea."

"Do you think that Lord Beaumont will have found the boat?"

"How should I know?" the Marquis replied sharply, and she knew he was still angry with her for having joined him.

They walked on in silence. Lucretia wondered if their slower pace was due to the Marquis's consideration for her, or whether he himself would have proceeded more slowly had he been alone.

They walked and walked! Lucretia was determined that she would say no more until the Marquis wished to speak with her and she was even more determined that whatever happened, or however long it took them to escape, she would not complain.

He would expect her to do so, she reasoned with herself. After all he had not wanted her company and he was, she was certain, the type of man who would consider women a considerable nuisance unless they kept to their own sphere of life.

"And that is in his bed!" she thought wryly, remembering Lady Hester's soft and seductive voice and the suggestive silence in the parlour of the Inn while she kissed the Marquis.

Yet Lucretia consoled herself that, however incensed the Marquis might be with her, however much a nuisance she might prove to him, she had entirely on her own made possible their escape from the French soldiers.

That at least must be a point in her favour! At the same time she was well aware that the Marquis might claim that, had she not been with him, he might not have been apprehended in the churchyard!

Everything that had happened seemed to repeat and repeat itself in Lucretia's mind as she walked on and on beside the Marquis.

It was impossible to see where they were going, and soon her feet were wet, her stockings torn to ribbons, and her legs had begun to ache almost painfully.

At last, when she had lost all reckoning of time, they came to what appeared in the darkness to be a large wood and the Marquis, speaking after what seemed to Lucretia hours of silence, said:

"I think we can go no further until dawn."

"I should have thought it was impossible for anyone to see us at the moment," Lucretia answered.

"Of that we cannot be sure," the Marquis replied, "so we will find a place to rest inside the wood. Follow me."

He moved as he spoke towards the black darkness of the trees which Lucretia could barely see in outline against the dark of the sky itself.

She followed him quickly, suddenly afraid that he might disappear and she would be left alone.

She realised he was feeling his way with his hands in front of him, and finally after a little while he said:

"The ground is sandy; I should think it will prove as comfortable as anything else on which we could seat ourselves."

He felt around with his hands and then said in a tone of satisfaction:

"There is even a fallen tree against which we can rest our backs."

"In fact every possible luxury!" Lucretia said with a hint of laughter in her voice.

It suddenly seemed to her almost funny that the Marquis with his great possessions, with Merlyncourt as his background, and she with her enormous fortune, should be scrabbling about in a French wood! Grateful for a fallen tree to support their weary limbs and talking of the comfort of some sandy ground!

The Marquis straightened himself and then by his movements she realised he was taking off his coat.

"What are you doing?" she asked.

"Put this on," he said, "you are going to find it chilly."

"But I cannot take your coat!" she expostulated.

"Why not?" he asked.

"I do not want you to catch cold," she answered.

"Are you serious?" he enquired. "A fashionable lady, Lucretia, would demand my coat as her right!"

"I am not a fashionable lady," Lucretia retorted, "and this dress is quite warm."

"I am not prepared to argue," the Marquis replied firmly. "And may I suggest that any lady, fashionable

127

or otherwise, Lucretia, would have the common sense to realise that the closer we sit together the warmer we are likely to be."

"I will not argue about that," she answered.

She put on the coat that he held out for her, and then she felt his arm guide her until she was sitting down beside him. Her back was against the fallen tree, her feet were stretched out in front of her on the sandy ground.

She was close against him. She could not see him, but she could hear every breath he drew and if she turned her head, her cheek brushed his shoulder.

After a moment she said:

"Will we get away?"

"We will do our damndest," the Marquis answered, "but naturally, like everything else in life, it depends on luck."

"And your luck is proverbial!"

"On previous occasions I have only had to worry about myself."

There was silence, and then Lucretia said in a small voice:

"Are you still . . . angry with me?"

"I was very angry indeed," the Marquis admitted after a moment. "But it is hard to be incensed with a woman who had the quick wit to rescue us both from what would have proved a very unpleasant military interrogation."

Lucretia gave a sigh of relief. She knew by his tone that he was in fact no longer even annoyed with her.

"And do you think Major Le Cloud—whoever he may be—would have been suspicious?"

"I think he would not have taken the risk in releasing us," the Marquis answered. "The French are obsessed by the idea that English have spies everywhere. I should imagine our chances of not being taken to Paris were very slender."

"And what do we do now?" Lucretia asked.

"We make every effort to rejoin the yacht. The Captain will sail to the other side of the peninsula to a place where I had told him to meet me if anything went wrong. It is just a matter of what lies in between."

Lucretia gave a little shiver. It was of fear, but the Marquis said quickly:

"Are you cold?"

Putting his arm round her he pulled her close, and now her head was resting on his chest.

He was wearing only a thin linen shirt and she could hear his heart beating steadily. The sound of it told her that she need not be afraid. Somehow in the miraculous manner in which he had won through before, the Marquis would get them both to safety.

"If I look up my lips would be near his," she thought.

The memory of his kiss in the barn made a thrill run through her, so that she drew in her breath.

"Shall I express my gratitude?" the Marquis asked softly, above her head.

"For what?" Lucretia enquired.

"For your ingenuity in contriving to knock out two Frenchmen in a very professional manner."

"I thought first when I went into the room with the Officer that I should have to knife him," Lucretia said. "But the knives were old and worn and I felt I would not have the strength to thrust one through his uniform."

"The method you chose was far more effective," the Marquis said. "I could hardly believe it was happening. I have never before had the privilege of seeing an Amazon in action."

"I was . . . frightened," Lucretia admitted.

"One is always frightened at times like that," the Marquis answered, "and yet there is an exhilaration in attempting the impossible."

"At least we are free for the . . . moment," Lucretia faltered.

His arm tightened round her and suddenly she thought to herself that the danger did not matter nor the discomfort, nor the fact that tomorrow might bring rearrest and perhaps the penalty of being shot as a spy.

All that was of importance was that she was close against him, that she could hear his heart, and that he was being kind to her.

"I love you, I love you," she wanted to say aloud.

But she knew that, if she were to do so, it would spoil this new comradeship, a feeling of togetherness that she had never known with him before.

This was not a moment for love, this was a moment of sharing a common danger, of being two people isolated in a foreign country against a common enemy.

"Try to sleep," she heard the Marquis say gently. "We have a very long day ahead of us tomorrow."

Lucretia thought it would be impossible to sleep, but she must have dozed a little because long before she expected it, a faint glow in the sky made it possible to see dimly the branches over their heads and the outline of the tree-trunks.

Finally they could see themselves as the Marquis drew Lucretia to her feet.

"We must go on," he said. "Are you all right?"

"Of course," she answered.

He rubbed his arms, untensed his shoulders, and she wondered if he was very stiff from holding her for so long.

"Please take your coat," she said. "It is too heavy for me to walk in . . . but thank you."

The Marquis took the coat from her shoulders. She wondered if he would notice as he put it on that it held the warmth from her body.

"You smell of violets," he said unexpectedly.

She remembered then that she had changed in such a hurry to leave the yacht that she had not used the exotic French perfume which she had thought to be in keeping with her sophisticated gowns.

Instead she had picked up the scent she preferred which was made especially for her by a perfumer in Jermyn Street.

"Do you like it?" she asked wondering if she had made a mistake.

"It haunted me for hours last night until I recognised the fragrance," he replied.

Lucretia wished she could see the expression on the Marquis's face. She felt uncertain what he was thinking or what she could say. Then abruptly he said:

"Come along, we must not waste time!"

They came out from the wood and walked along the side of it, being able to see very little because a morning mist lay over the fields.

They must have walked for nearly an hour before they came to another wood. The Marquis entered it and, following a path which twisted and turned between the trunks of the trees, they finally emerged on the other side, to see lying before them a valley of open fields without a tree in sight.

"I thought I was not mistaken," the Marquis said as if speaking to himself. "This is where it will be dangerous."

"Why?" Lucretia asked.

"Because we shall have to move in the open," he answered. "There are no woods in which we can take cover."

He stood looking into the valley, and now, as it grew lighter and the first faint glow of the sun appeared in the East, Lucretia saw that directly below them was a small farm house.

It was poor and rough but there was smoke coming from one of the chimneys, and even as she stood looking at it, out from the door came three people.

There were two women and a man. They were all carrying farm implements, and Lucretia knew they were going into the fields to start work.

One woman seemed bowed with age, the other was obviously younger. But the man was moving slower than they were and Lucretia realised he was limping.

The Marquis was watching them too. Unexpectedly he said:

"Stay here. Keep in the shadow of the trees and if you see anyone coming, hide."

"Where are you going?" Lucretia asked. "You are not leaving me?"

She felt a sudden fear of being alone.

"I am going to see what I can find," the Marquis answered, "and primarily something for breakfast."

Lucretia looked towards the three people who had

come from the farm. They were moving into the morning mist and becoming indistinct.

"Is it safe?" she asked anxiously.

"I will be careful," the Marquis answered with a smile.

He said no more but bending low moved towards the farm. Lucretia stood in the shadow of the trees watching him.

She had no idea what he was about to do or what he expected to find. Breakfast of any sort would be very welcome, she suddenly realised she was hungry and she was certain that the Marquis was too.

She saw him reach the farm and without hesitating go to the door. He disappeared and she supposed he must have entered the building or perhaps someone let him in.

Suddenly she felt terror-struck. Supposing there were men waiting inside to capture him? Supposing he never returned?

"I am being nonsensical," she told herself, but at the same time she knew that the terror she had felt for the Marquis was because she loved him.

On calm reflection it was unlikely there would be anyone left in the farm except perhaps a man or woman too aged to work in the fields.

Peasants were very industrous, as Lucretia knew. At this time of year they would all be out at dawn. Even children helped in harvesting.

But however sensible and logical it might be to assume he was walking into an empty farmhouse, it was quite a different thing when it concerned someone she loved.

She could not rid herself of visions of soldiers lying in wait for the Marquis or of him being felled from behind by a blow on the head.

"Keep him safe, please God keep him safe!" she prayed and went on praying.

When she opened her eyes, she saw him returning. He was carrying a large bundle in his arms and she could not think what is could be until he had actually reached her side.

"What is that?" she asked, hardly conscious that she was speaking, so anxiously were her eyes searching his face for confirmation that all was well.

He smiled at her.

"I have brought our disguises with me," he said, "and the sooner we change into them the better."

"What are they?" she asked curiously.

"Quite a pretty dress for you," he answered. "I am afraid it must be Madame's Sunday best!"

He handed her a number of garments as he spoke and then he looked down at what he held in his arms.

"And for me," he said slowly, "a uniform of one of the Emperor's most faithful warriors."

Lucretia looked in astonishment and saw the blue and white coat of a French regiment.

"You cannot wear that!" she gasped.

The Marquis gave a little laugh.

"I would wear the horns and tail of the devil himself to get us safely to the yacht," he answered. "Hurry and change, Lucretia. The sooner we are away from here the better. And then if you are a good girl I will give you something to eat."

He spoke jestingly as one might to a child, but Lucretia knew that the order was given in earnest and without argument she went further into the wood, put down the clothes he had given her and started to take off her gown.

She realised he had been right in thinking it was "Madame's Sunday best." There was the red camlet jacket which all the peasant women wore, the full cotton petticoats, and a high white apron.

The Marquis had even remembered the stiff white cap with its long flying lappets.

The clothes were well-worn but they were clean, and Lucretia guessed that the Marquis must have found them folded away carefully in a drawer.

They were too large for her, especially round the waist, but she managed to knot the apron at the neck and she plaited her hair neatly beneath the cap as she had seen the French women do.

She pushed her expensive gown down a rabbit hole

133

and went back to the Marquis. He was sitting down cutting away with his knife at the toe-cap of a leather boot.

"What on earth are you doing?" she asked.

"At moments like this it is a damn nuisance being so big. Fortunately no-one would be surprised if any French soldier showed his toes and Napoleon, as we all know, has not the money to spend on smart uniforms."

"They will be uncomfortable," Lucretia warned.

"I have something far more uncomfortable for you," he answered.

He glanced to one side as he spoke and she saw that lying on the ground beside him was a pair of wooden sabots.

"Have I to wear those?" she enquired.

"Only if we see anyone coming," he answered. "They are agony to walk in. I suggest you carry them and slip them on if we have to go through a village, or if by any misfortune we meet some French citizens with curious eyes."

He finished cutting loose the front of the boots and put them on, tying them with broken shoe-laces. He was wearing a pair of torn and tattered breeches which had undoubtedly endured a lot of hard wear.

The Marquis stood up.

"Have you discarded your chemise?"

"No," Lucretia answered in surprise, "should I have done so?"

The Marquis smiled.

"I think, if we are interrogated, they might be rather surprised to find a French peasant wearing silk and lace next to her skin. However, if you are to hang, I may as well hang with you and keep my own shirt! The gentleman who wore this tunic was, I gather, a good healthy smelling son of the soil."

"I will throw away my chemise if you want me to do so," Lucretia said.

"Do not bother," the Marquis answered. "We must just be careful not to get ourselves caught."

He put on the soldier's tunic as he spoke over his

134

own shirt. It was too small for him and too narrow across the shoulders. It was so torn and battered that when the Marquis split several seams to make himself more comfortable, there was no noticeable difference.

"And now," he said to Lucretia, "you tell me you have worked in a hospital so you can make a bandage out of that towel and put it round my head."

She picked up the towel from the ground where it lay beside the wooden clogs, and while the Marquis took his discarded clothes and disappeared into the wood with them, she tore it into the right shape.

The towel which was of cheap cotton had been rough dried and it looked already rather worn and grubby.

"Are you ready for me?" the Marquis inquired coming back through the trees.

"Sit down," Lucretia said.

He did as he was told and she put the bandage round his forehead and tied it in an expert manner at the back of his head.

"How do I look?" he asked his eyes twinkling.

"Exactly as I should expect a French Dandy to appear," she answered, "and I hope, Monsieur, I am *chic* enough to accompany you."

His eyes flickered over her. The white cap was very becoming on her dark hair, and her anxious blue eyes seemed almost too big for her small face.

"Très élégante!" the Marquis said, "and now let us hurry. When we are nearly a mile away I promise you a crust of bread and some liver-sausage."

"Your hospitality overwhelms me!" Lucretia replied.

She picked up the clogs and slung them over her shoulder.

The Marquis had attached them to each other by a lace from his discarded shoes and she knew it would be easier to carry them that way than over her arm.

Even so they were quite heavy and she feared that before the end of the day she was going to find them a wearisome burden.

At the same time she was well aware the Marquis

had an eye for detail which was extremely important in the situation in which they found themselves.

No Frenchwoman of the peasant class would in war time be rich enough to afford to buy shoes and clogs were therefore essential for her disguise.

They walked past the farm and out into the open country.

"If we do meet anyone who speaks to us," the Marquis said, "I shall pretend to be stupid and dazed from the wound in my head. You will explain that I have been discharged from the Army and you are taking me home to my parents who live at Les Pieux."

"Is that where we are going?" Lucretia asked.

"Near it," he replied.

"Is it a long way?"

"It is going to take us all today and perhaps part of tomorrow," he said, "but we dare not go anywhere near the coast until almost the last minute."

"I thought you would make a big detour," Lucretia exclaimed.

A little further on, she said:

"I feel rather mean, taking these clothes from those people . . . they are so poor and have to work so hard!"

There was a pause and then as if he did not want to tell her, the Marquis said:

"I left them some money!"

"You did!" Lucretia exclaimed. "But will it not make them suspicious that it was not an ordinary theft?"

"I thought of that," the Marquis said, "so I used the old trick of smashing a china tea-pot and tucking several franc notes into the broken pieces."

"So when they find it, they will imagine it must have been forgotten for ages . . . perhaps years," Lucretia cried.

"It is easier to do it with books," the Marquis said, "but these people do not read."

They walked on. After a time Lucretia said softly:

"You know the trouble with you is that you have a soft heart."

"Nonsense!" the Marquis replied. "As you will find,

136

Lucretia, if you try any more tricks, I am both rough and tough."

"So tough that you give your money to the enemy and your coat to a tiresome woman," Lucretia answered.

"Can you be turning me into a hero?" the Marquis asked in an amused voice.

"Why not?" Lucretia replied, "so long as I can play the heroine! But alas, I suspect there are a large number of applicants for the part!"

"Let us stop here and eat," the Marquis suggested. "My powers of repartee are not as their brightest so early in the morning.

He had brought from the farm almost a whole loaf of dark black bread. It was rather sour and unpleasant in taste, but Lucretia knew without being told that it was very nourishing.

The liver sausage was full of garlic. She wrinkled her nose.

"It is a good thing we are both eating this," she said, "or tonight one of us would certainly be unwilling to sleep close to the other."

"Were you anticipating we should?" the Marquis asked.

She gave him a mischievious glance.

"Are you bored with me already as a sleeping companion," she questioned. "I could not imagine you could be so fickle! On the other hand perhaps I should have anticipated it."

"Are you still trying to provoke me, Lucretia?" he enquired.

"What other amusements are there at the moment?" she asked wide-eyed. "I must commend you, My Lord, on providing, if nothing else, a very original honeymoon!"

He looked at her for a moment, watching her white teeth bite into the thick black bread and noting the sparkle in her eyes even though she had not rested more than a few hours during the night.

"What sort of honeymoon would you prefer?" he asked unexpectedly.

She glanced at him quickly, trying to think of a pert and amusing reply. Then suddenly, almost without her conscious volition, she spoke the truth.

"To be with someone I . . . loved and who loved . . . me."

There was a moments silence before the Marquis said:

"If you have finished this delectable meal, Lucretia, I think we should be moving on."

"But of course, My Lord," she replied lightly, "the carriage waits."

She wondered as they walked over the next field what he thought of her answer to his question. Then with a constriction of her heart she wondered if he too would have liked a honeymoon with someone he loved. Would he be happy now if he had Lady Hester beside him?

Of one thing she was quite sure, that had her Ladyship been with him last night they would have made love in the darkness of the wood!

Involuntarily Lucretia gave a little sigh.

"Are you all right?" the Marquis asked.

She thought that his tone was anxious.

"But of course," she replied. "I am just wondering how soon your boots are going to give you blisters on your feet."

"My feet are pretty hard," the Marquis answered. "But at the same time I admit to preferring my hessians."

"And of course the champagne with which to polish them," Lucretia quipped.

"Talking of champagne," the Marquis said, "I am thirsty, as I am sure you are. Let us hope we find a spring. It would not be safe to drink standing water."

It was two hours before they found one and by that time Lucretia was beginning to think that her lips would crack and that her voice was growing hoarse in her throat.

But the spring was bubbling out of the ground into a small pool. They drank at the source, cupping their hands for the water and lifting it eagerly to their lips.

138

"I have never tasted anything so delicious!" Lucretia exclaimed.

"I agree with you," the Marquis replied. "I would not change that drink for a pipe of the finest port."

Lucretia dipped her hands and arms into the cool water and then washed her face. As she did so she remembered she had no cosmetics to make herself look alluring, nothing to accentuate the mystery of her eyes.

Metaphorically she shrugged her shoulders. It was impossible at this moment to try to appear sophisticated! Anyhow the Marquis would be too concerned in trying to reach the yacht to find her anything but a hindrance.

The Marquis also washed his face and poured water over his head. Lucretia readjusted the bandage and they were off again.

They walked on, and now Lucretia was beginning to find, as she had anticipated, that the clogs were very heavy to carry.

She said nothing but suddenly the Marquis lifted them from her shoulders.

"Forgive me, Lucretia," he said, "I should have thought of this before."

"You cannot carry them," she said quickly. "Supposing someone sees you?"

"We must take care they do not," he replied.

They trudged on through the heat of the day and the bandage around the Marquis's head making him, Lucretia knew, very hot, while she began to find her white linen cap was tight and uncomfortable.

As they came through a long green field of barley they saw ahead of them a small hamlet, and stopped as they were about to cross a small dusty road.

"We had best go north of the village I think," the Marquis said.

Lucretia saw that this meant once again going over a number of fields that had been ploughed, where the walking was far more tiring than when they moved over grass.

"Can we rest for a . . . moment?" she asked.

139

It was the first time she had suggested it, and the Marquis said in consternation:

"I should have asked before if you wished to do so. I am sorry, Lucretia, and I am being extraordinarily inconsiderate."

"You are nothing of the sort," Lucretia answered. "I know women are a nuisance at a time like this. I am trying very hard to make you forget that I am one."

"That would be impossible," the Marquis replied.

She wondered if he was paying her a compliment and then decided against it. Instead she sat down gratefully on the roadside, feeling that her feet would carry her no further.

The Marquis put the clogs down beside her, and stretched out his legs in front of him.

"I wonder if I dare take off this damn bandage?" he said.

"Let me make it narrower," Lucretia suggested.

"It would not look so effective," he objected.

"You should not think so much about your appearance," she teased him. "It is a good thing there are not many women about: you know that the poor wounded soldier act always appeals to the softness of a feminine heart."

The Marquis was just about to answer her when there was a sound of voices.

Quickly Lucretia slipped off her own shoes and put her feet into the wooden clogs.

She had hardly done so when round the corner of the road which led towards the hamlet came two soldiers.

Their uniforms were nearly as disreputable as that worn by the Marquis, but had caps on their heads and one soldier had his arm round the other's shoulder.

As they came nearer Lucretia realised they were both drunk. They were walking unsteadily laughing with each other and one of them broke into a little song just before they saw Lucretia and the Marquis.

They came staggering up to them.

"*Bonjour Comrade,*" one of them exclaimed.

The Marquis did not answer. With his shoulders

hunched and his head sunk forward on his chest, he was staring down at his feet in the roadway.

"He's been wounded in the head," Lucretia explained, "he cannot answer you."

"*Quel mal chance!* But he's lucky to have you to look after him," one of the soldiers remarked.

He appeared to be trying to focus his drunken eyes on her.

"*Qui, très,*" Lucretia agreed, "but we must not keep you from wherever you are going."

"Come on, Jacques," the other soldier said.

"*Je viens,*" Jacques answered.

"Poor wounded devil!" he said. "That's war for you—destroys a man one way or another."

"Come on," the other soldier urged again.

"But he's fortunate to have you," his drunken friend Jacques repeated to Lucretia. "Fortunate, very fortunate."

His friend gave him a tug and he started to stagger away down the road. Lucretia watched them apprehensively.

"Deserters," the Marquis said almost beneath his breath.

"How do you know?" she asked.

"There are thousands of them all over the country," the Marquis replied.

The two soldiers had gone a little way down the road, but now they had stopped and were talking to each other.

Lucretia wondered what they were saying, and then suddenly they came staggering back.

They seemed by the expression on their faces to have come to some agreement with each other. Jacques appeared to be a little the more sober.

When they reached Lucretia and the Marquis she looked up, an anxious expression in her eyes.

"What is it?" she enquired.

"He's no use to you," Jacques replied pointing at the Marquis, "not with a hole in his head. You come along with us. We'll look after you."

"No thank you," Lucretia answered, "this is my man . . . my husband. I am taking him to Les Pieux to his parents. He'll get better there."

"Or he'll die," Jacques said. "You don't want to waste your time with him. You're a pretty girl and we like pretty girls, don't we Paul?"

"Yes," Paul answered, "we like pretty girls, and you're very pretty, *chérie*."

As he spoke he put out his hand towards Lucretia. She shrank a little closer to the Marquis.

"Go away!" she said fiercely. "I want nothing to do with either of you! This is my husband and I am staying with him. *Allez-vous-en!*"

"You're coming with us!" Paul told her roughly.

He was an older man with a scarred ugly face and thick lips and there was a glint in his eye which told her that he was more dangerous than Jacques.

He bent down and took Lucretia by the arm.

"Come on now," he said, "we haven't had a woman for a week and we never thought to find one as pretty as you."

"*Non, non!*" Lucretia cried with a tremor of fear in her voice.

Then the Marquis acted.

For a moment it was difficult for Lucretia to see exactly what had happened, and certainly the two drunken Frenchmen could have had little memory of what had actually occurred.

The Marquis hit Jacques first because he was the nearest. He gave him an uppercut on the chin which almost lifted him off his feet and he fell senseless in the road.

Paul had time to see what was happening. He relinquished his hold on Lucretia and turning raised his clenched fist to strike the Marquis, but he was too slow.

The Marquis hit him twice and he too was unconscious.

It seemed to Lucretia that there was a smile of sheer satisfaction on the Marquis's face as he looked at his two fallen adversaries. Then he took Lucretia by the hand as if she was a child and led her into a field which skirted the village.

They moved steadily but without undue hurry until they were out of sight of the road and the two unconscious soldiers.

CHAPTER 8

They walked for some way before Lucretia said in a low voice, almost as if she spoke to herself:

"I did not ... know that ... men were like ... that."

She was thinking of the lewd expression in Paul's eyes, the thickness of his lips and the manner in which he put out his hand to grasp at her arm.

She knew that, if the Marquis had not been with her, she would have been frightened as she had never before been frightened in her whole life.

"Like what?" the Marquis enquired.

"That they ... wanted a ... woman simply because ... she was ... a woman," Lucretia answered, trying to find words to express her thoughts. "That was why those soldiers were asking me to ... go with them ... was it not? So that they could ... make ... love to me?"

There was a moment's silence, and then the Marquis said with a jeering note in his voice:

"Has not your lover—or lovers—explained such matters to you?"

As he spoke he looked at Lucretia and saw the colour rush into her face and recede again, leaving her curiously pale.

He felt as if he had struck something small, soft and vulnerable, and after a brief hesitation, he said in a very different tone:

"Shall I try and explain it to you, Lucretia?"

She did not reply, but her fingers trembled in his and she would have taken her hand away had he not held it so tightly.

144

"Making love," the Marquis said slowly as if he was feeling for words, "is an expression that is used to cover a multitude of emotions. A man may feel desire, passion, infatuation or lust for a woman, Lucretia, but none of these things are love."

She did not speak, but he knew she was listening intently.

"When a man really loves a woman," the Marquis went on, "he will desire her body—that is natural—but he will want to possess her heart also and perhaps her soul. And when they are together, when they 'make love', as it is called, then it is something much more than merely physical, it is a rapture and a joy which is also mental and spiritual.

"It is an ecstasy which carries them both towards the burning heart of the sun, and for which there is no words."

His voice died away. Then he said very quietly:

"That is real love, Lucretia, which all men seek and long for."

Lucretia felt herself quiver at the note in the Marquis's voice which seemed to vibrate through her whole body.

Then, with a sudden sinking of her heart, she supposed that the ecstasy of which he spoke was what he felt for Lady Hester.

He must love her because she was so beautiful, and the reason he did not marry her was that he could not afford to do so.

She knew that the Marquis was waiting for her to speak, and after a moment she said hesitatingly:

"Thank you for . . . telling me."

"Look at me, Lucretia!" he said unexpectedly, and obediently she turned her face up to his.

He looked down into her eyes. They were puzzled and very innocent—the eyes of a child.

"You were right, Lucretia, in what you said to me the night we were married," the Marquis said softly. "You must never 'make love' with a man unless he loves you with all his heart and you love him in the same way."

145

Again his voice made her quiver with a strange unaccountable feeling that she had never known before.

Then because she was shy, because she had never expected the Marquis to speak to her in such a manner, she dropped her eyes and saw that his hand with which he was holding hers was bleeding.

He had broken the skin of his knuckles when he hit first Jacques and then Paul.

"Your hand!" she exclaimed. "You must have hurt yourself!"

"It is nothing," the Marquis said relinquishing her fingers.

He would have wiped the blood away with a handkerchief which he pulled from his pocket, but Lucretia put out her hand and stopped him.

"Your handkerchief is dirty," she said, "it might infect the wound. I must find something clean with which to cover it."

"You are molly-coddling me," the Marquis said with a smile, "it will be quite all right."

"No, we must not take chances," Lucretia contradicted. "Supposing you ran a fever?"

She stood looking at his hand as if she was wondering what to do, until she said suddenly:

"Give me your knife."

The Marquis brought out his knife, opened it and held it out to her. She took it and said as if to herself:

"There is nothing else."

She turned her back on him and pulled up her full petticoats. It was difficult to hack away a part of her chemise but she managed it, and then pulling down her skirts she turned back towards the Marquis.

"This is cleaner than anything else we have."

He looked at the long strip of pure white silk and then at the serious expression on Lucretia's face, but he said nothing and merely put out his hand and allowed her to bandage his knuckles.

"If we find another spring," she said, "I will wash it to be quite sure it is clean."

"I bow to your expert medical knowledge," the Marquis said.

"It may seem fussy to you," Lucretia answered, "but a great many of the wounds that I saw in the hospital in Paris were aggravated by dirt and flies."

"Your training is now proving unexpectedly useful," the Marquis smiled.

Lucretia thought he was teasing her and as they started to walk on again she said:

"I would not wish you to think that I was boasting unduly when I told you that I worked in the hospital. I was not of course allowed to attend to any of the patients alone, but only to help the Nuns with the cleaning of wounds and re-bandaging. I was also restricted to being with the Nun who attended the blind and those with head wounds."

"I think you are being scrupulously honest in not claiming too much glory," the Marquis answered.

"I should not wish there to be any pretence between us, My Lord."

Then as Lucretia spoke she thought how many pretences in fact there were already—the pretence that she was sophisticated, the pretence that other men had loved her, the pretence that she was a woman-of-the-world, ready to cross swords in repartee with the Marquis and try to defeat him in a duel of words.

Suddenly she saw Paul's lustful eyes devouring her and felt lost and afraid.

What did she know about men? What did she know about the Marquis except that she loved him? And she was so ignorant of all the things that he must find interesting and fascinating in a sophisticated woman.

Once again Lucretia saw herself outside the gates of Merlyncourt, peering through them but unable to get in. An outsider!

"How can I compete with Lady Hester?" she asked herself, "with her fabulous beauty, her soft seductive lips which the Marquis must long to kiss?"

Did he not feel when he was with Lady Hester the ecstasy and rapture of which he had just spoken? And if he did, how could she ever hope to win him and his love?

147

They walked on and it seemed that the Marquis too was deep in his own thoughts.

They crossed field after field. They saw peasants working on the crops but they managed to avoid coming into contact with any of them.

Lucretia began to feel hungry, but she was determined not to say so, not to be the first to admit to any discomfort.

She knew from the way the Marquis was walking that his split boots, as she had anticipated, were causing blisters on his feet, and she knew that the soles of her own feet were growing sorer every mile.

At least it was better than wearing the clogs which once again the Marquis was carrying on his shoulder.

But Lucretia was beginning to wonder how many more miles it was to the other side of the peninsula.

They were lucky in that there was no sign of any soldiers. This was an agricultural region and bar a few isolated farm-buildings and several small hamlets they saw nothing but fields of corn, of roots and mustard.

"Are you hungry?" the Marquis asked when they must have walked in silence for nearly half an hour.

"I was just wondering if the rumbling I heard was your tummy or mine, or perhaps distant thunder," Lucretia replied with a smile.

He laughed.

"Three good meals a day are not the right training for a long-distance walk."

"I was just thinking of our friends who probably were sitting down an hour or so ago to a big meal and complaining there was really nothing fit to eat."

"I am afraid my mind was wondering to the Dining-room table at Carlton House," the Marquis said. "Twenty-five entrées at one dinner and buffets for the Prince's Receptions loaded with food until one wondered the tables did not collapse beneath them."

"Thinking of food makes you all the hungrier!" Lucretia said.

"I know that," the Marquis replied, "but it is an extraordinary thing, and I have experienced this before, how difficult it is to have lofty thoughts on other sub-

148

jects when you feel as if you have a hole in your belly."

"A most indelicate expression, My Lord!" Lucretia laughed.

"If only it were later in the season, there might be some fruit," the Marquis said.

Lucretia turned her face towards him with a light in her eyes.

"You have given me an idea," she said. "Let us walk along the edge of the next field we have to cross."

The Marquis did as she suggested, and sure enough after they had searched for a little while they found some wild strawberries, small and sweet *fraises des bois*.

"Ambrosia of the gods!" the Marquis exclaimed.

"But the gods are regrettably stingy," Lucretia complained.

She would have gone on looking if the Marquis had not said firmly he dared not waste much time.

"We still have a long way to go," he said, "and we have to find somewhere to sleep tonight."

"In the open?" Lucretia asked.

"I have never seen land with so little cover," the Marquis remarked with a note of irritation in his voice.

They walked on and on, and Lucretia found it increasingly difficult to talk. She was conscious of the fact that the Marquis was deliberately slowing his pace so that she would not have to exert herself.

"I am an encumbrance on him," she thought despairingly. He must be resenting her because she was a hindrance since if he had been alone he would have been able to cover the ground twice as quickly.

They found a spring from which they could drink and Lucretia insisted on the Marquis washing his hand.

She saw however that the broken skin of his knuckles looked clean and she guessed that with his tremendously good health there was really no danger.

But because she enjoyed doing it for him, she put back the silk bandage and adjusted it neatly around his hand.

"Is your head quite comfortable?" she asked.

"It is all right," the Marquis answered. "I dislike having to say it, Lucretia, but we must not linger or waste time. The French will perhaps guess that we have moved further round the coast, in which case the sooner we reach the yacht at Les Priex the safer it will be."

"Yes, of course I understand," Lucretia said getting up obediently from beside the spring.

They started off again and she walked as quickly as she could, but by the time the sun had lost its heat and the afternoon was drawing in she did feel desperately tired.

It was then that the Marquis, looking down at her pale resolute little face, said:

"I have made a decision. The next really isolated farm-house we come to, you will knock on the door and ask for shelter for the night."

"Will it be safe?" Lucretia asked.

"As safe as wandering about in the open," he answered. "You must explain that I have been wounded, and it is best if I hardly speak at all. The countryside is full of deserters scavenging all they can, robbing the peasants and making a general nuisance of themselves. A farmer would refuse us shelter if he thought I was one of those men."

"I will do all the talking," Lucretia agreed. "Do you think my assumed accent is convincing?"

"It still sounds rather ladylike," the Marquis said, "but I must commend you, Lucretia, on your French."

"And I am very surprised how good yours is," she answered.

"I was well taught when I was young," the Marquis replied, "and I have taken a great many lessons in the last two years from émegrés who crossed the Channel after the Revolution."

"It was a wise thing to do, considering the task you had set yourself in helping so many Englishmen escape from France."

"It was an act of self-preservation," the Marquis replied. "When one is disguised, a word used in the wrong sense or spoken in a careless manner can mean the difference between, if not life and death, certainly freedom or imprisonment."

Lucretia shuddered.

"I do not like to think of your taking such risks."

The Marquis smiled.

"What about you? What risks are you taking at this moment?"

"You had to have someone to look after you," she teased, "otherwise Major Le Cloud would undoubtedly by now have brought you before the Tribunal."

"But of course," the Marquis agreed, "and perhaps one day I shall be able to thank you."

"Let us hope that very soon we shall be in the position to thank each other," Lucretia said. "For the moment I have the uneasy feeling I may die of starvation beside the road."

The Marquis stood still and looked around him.

"There is a farm," he said pointing towards the horizon. "It appears to stand by itself. Let us make for it, Lucretia. If nothing else, it will be a relief to take off these cursed boots."

Lucretia managed the half mile which led to the farm with a renewed energy.

She found herself thinking that any food, however bad, however scanty, would be palatable and even enjoyable.

The farm when they reached it was larger than it had seemed in the distance and was built in the usual French fashion with a barn, a byre, an open yard, all adjoining the house itself.

As they went up to the door, Lucretia's eyes met those of the Marquis.

"Courage," he said very softly, "and keep your fingers crossed!"

"They are," she whispered.

They knocked on the door and for a moment there was only silence. Then they heard footsteps coming across a flagged floor.

The door opened and an elderly peasant-woman stood there. She had an old weather-beaten skin leathery from long exposure to the sun and wind. Her hair was grey, but her eyes, while a little apprehensive, were kind.

"*Pardon, Madame*," Lucretia began. "But I wonder if you would be kind enough to grant my husband and me shelter for tonight. We have walked a long way and, if you cannot accommodate us in the house, perhaps we might rest in one of your barns."

The French woman looked at the Marquis. She took in the bandage round his head, his shoulders sagging in fatigue, the burst front of his army boots.

"*Hélas!* Your man is wounded!" she exclaimed.

"In the head, *Madame*. He has been very ill and he is still stupid. He doesn't realise what is going on. But we are trying to reach his parents who live in Les Priex. He will be able to rest there."

"It is a long way," the woman said. "Come in, come in, both of you. You can sit by the fire, it is growing chill."

She turned and Lucretia and the Marquis followed her into a flagged kitchen which had an oak-beamed ceiling and a fireplace in which was burning a small fire. There was a table of heavy wood, some simple chairs and a dresser.

The ceiling was very low, and Lucretia thought that if the Marquis had stood upright his head would have struck the beams.

"You look tired," the woman said. "Have you come far?"

"A long way, *Madame*," Lucretia answered. "My husband was discharged, and as always with the Army they are not interested what happens to you afterwards."

"That's true!" the woman said. "What are our men but cannon-fodder?"

She spoke so bitterly that Lucretia asked:

"You have lost someone you loved, *Madame*?"

"My husband and two of my sons," the woman replied. "There is one left, but I haven't heard from him for six months."

"I am sorry," Lucretia said feeling somehow that words were inadequate. "But how do you manage?"

152

"I have a nephew who lives in a village three miles away. He comes over and sees to the crops when he can spare the time from his own farm. But it is hard, very hard without a man to help, and without a man to care for."

The woman's voice broke. Then with an effort she said:

"But you must be hungry. When did you last eat?"

"This morning, *Madame*. And we can pay for what you can spare us."

"That's not important," the woman said. "But I must see what I can find you. Would you and your man care for an omelette?"

"We would indeed," Lucretia said unable to prevent her voice sounding almost over-elated.

"I'll see what the hens have laid," the woman said and went from the kitchen.

Lucretia did not dare speak to the Marquis in case their hostess was listening, but she put out her hand and took his.

She felt the warm pressure of his fingers and once again her spirits rose.

This was comradeship. They were in this together, they shared every little victory, and because of it they were close.

The French woman came shuffling back into the kitchen. Lucretia had put on her clogs before they reached the farm and she thought as she heard their hostess approach that there was certainly one thing about them, that no-one who wore them could creep upon them unawares.

"You're in luck," the French woman said. "Five eggs, newly laid! My hens must have known you were coming!"

"But *Madame*, we must not take all your food."

The woman smiled.

"It's nice to have company. *Hélas*, I'm so much alone! Sometimes I go a week without speaking to anyone. I see my nephew in the field but he doesn't always come to the house."

She put the eggs down on the table and went to get a pan and a basin from the dresser.

"Let me help you," Lucretia said.

"I think there's some bread in the larder," the woman answered, "and cheese. I make my own from goat's milk. And there should be butter too. I used to be famous in the market for my butter and cheese, but its too far for me to walk there now. They took my horse away soon after the war started."

"That was hard," Lucretia remarked.

"Hard!" the woman exclaimed. "Everything about war is hard! I thought to live here with my husband in peace until I died. He was too old to fight, but they insisted that they could use him. And my sons one went after another. The youngest, who is still alive, is not yet seventeen."

There was so much agony in the French woman's voice that Lucretia felt she wanted to cry.

This was how war affected the ordinary people—the people who did not understand the cause for which they were forced to fight, who only knew that their quiet lives were shattered and destroyed, leaving in the end nothing but emptiness and memories.

"What's your name, *Madame?*" the French woman asked suddenly and Lucretia realised that she and the Marquis had not discussed what they should call themselves.

Then quickly she remembered the name he had given the soldier.

"Bouvais," she replied, "and that of course is the name of my husband's family in Les Priex."

"It is a well-known name," the woman said automatically as if she made a gesture of politeness. "And mine, *Madame*, is Croix."

"Then, *Madame* Croix, we must thank you for being so kind," Lucretia said with a smile. "My husband and I are very grateful."

Lucretia set the bread, butter and the cheese upon the table. She was glad to see there was three quarters of a loaf left and the cheese was large.

She could feel her mouth watering at the thought of

154

the omelette, and it was difficult to prevent herself from slicing a piece of the bread right away and pushing it into her mouth.

"I am afraid my coffee is a very poor quality," Madame Croix was saying. "We cannot get good coffee now. They tell me it's made of acorns, and the *Bon Dieu* knows that is what it tastes of. But we mix it with goat's milk. It's better that way."

Lucretia wanted to reply that to her it would taste better anyway, but she forced herself to find the plates, to ask Madame Croix where the knives and forks were kept, and finally to wait expectantly as her hostess folded over the omelette and fried it to exactly the right shade of brown.

"You will eat with us, *Madame?*" Lucretia asked.

"No thank you," the older woman said. "I ate at midday, and I find I don't sleep if I eat at night. Divide the omelette between yourself and your good man. I am sure you are in need of it."

She handed the pan to Lucretia as she spoke and busied herself with the coffee.

Lucretia cut the omelette and gave the Marquis at least three quarters. She set it on the plate and holding the pan high so that he could not see how little remained, took it across to him.

He had been sitting at the table with his head bent, but now she set the omelette down in front of him and said in a tone that one uses to a child:

"Eat up your food, Pierre, it will do you good. We still have a long way to go."

The Marquis obediently, and also because he was hungry, put his fork into the omelette and started to eat quickly.

Lucretia walked back towards the fire and only when the Marquis had finished did she tip from the pan the rest of the omelette on to her plate.

He saw what she had done and she thought for a moment he would have spoken. Then as she frowned at him to evoke caution, he said nothing.

She ate her portion of the omelette quickly, thinking

that nothing she had ever eaten before had tasted so good.

Almost like magic she felt with every mouthful her fatigue ebbing away and a buoyance coming back.

She sliced the bread, giving the Marquis the inner cut so that he would not have the outside, and passed him the butter and the goat's-milk cheese.

"I am afraid we shall leave you little in the house," she said apologetically to Madame Croix as she helped herself to a third piece of bread.

"You eat all you can," the French woman answered. "I need very little and the carrier comes tomorrow. I can get new provisions."

"Are you sure?" Lucretia asked.

"Quite sure, my dear," Madame Croix replied. "I only wish I had a stew to offer you, but it would take too long to kill a chicken."

"We are very grateful for what we have," Lucretia said in all sincerity.

The coffee and goat's milk was not very pleasant but it was hot and both she and the Marquis drank it gratefully.

In the warmth of the kitchen Lucretia found her eye-lids dropping and Madame Croix noticed it.

"Now you two go up to bed," she said. "It is fortunate that my best bedroom is ready, because there was a chance that my cousin might be coming to see me from St. Malo. That is not far from Les Priex by the way; she might know your husband's parents."

"You must ask her when she arrives," Lucretia said, "but I am glad she is not here tonight."

The French woman smiled.

"You can have her bed and you are welcome to it. The sheets are clean and, though I say it myself, there's not a more comfortable feather-bed in the whole of Brittany."

Lucretia thought that any bed would be like heaven after the way they had slept last night.

Madame Croix turned towards the narrow staircase. Lucretia hesitated.

"Would it be impolite to inquire, *Madame*," she

156

asked, "if there is a basin in the room? I would dearly like to wash."

"But of course," Madame Croix replied. "We will take up a bucket of water. The pump is outside in the yard."

"I will fill it," Lucretia said.

She walked outside to the pump, but as she lifted the heavy bucket she wondered if once it was filled, if she would be able to carry it. Even as she wondered about it she found the Marquis beside her.

"Careful!" she whispered warningly.

"Explain," he said almost beneath his breath, "that although I am half-witted, I can still carry things."

They went back into the kitchen.

"Pierre's getting better," Lucretia said lightly, "he understood that I wanted him to carry the bucket. He's quite bright at times."

"Do the doctors think he will regain all his faculties?" Madame Croix questioned.

"Doctors!" Lucretia ejaculated. "What they don't know would fill a thousand books. They said he might be better, but then on the other hand he might not. How can you believe them?"

"How indeed!" Madame Croix agreed mournfully.

She led the way up the stairs followed by Lucretia, and behind them came the Marquis carrying the heavy bucket of water.

The bedroom had a low ceiling, and although by now it was growing dusk it was easy to see one bed against the wall and a rough deal table holding an earthenware basin with another bucket under it.

There was a chair and a chest with a very small piece of looking-glass on top of it.

"Thank you very much, *Madame*," Lucretia said, "we are very grateful for your kindness."

"*Ce n'est rien de tout*," Madame Croix replied. "It is not only a Christian act to help those in need, but we cannot do too much for those who have been wounded in these terrible wars."

"No indeed," Lucretia said in a soft voice, "and I

157

am sorry, *Madame*, more than I can ever tell you, that you have lost so much."

"Three of them!" Madame Croix murmured, then she turned and went from the room.

They listened to her footsteps going down the stairs, and the Marquis straightened his back.

His eyes met Lucretia's across the small room, and for a few moments neither of them spoke.

"Are you going to suggest," he asked at length, "that if I were a gentleman I should sleep on the floor tonight?"

"No, of course not!" Lucretia said quickly. "You are as tired as I am. We will put a pillow between us."

"I might have known," the Marquis said, "that you would offer an eminently practical solution to what might have proved a somewhat difficult problem."

"There is no difficulty about it," Lucretia said in a matter-of-fact voice. "And now, if you will sit on the chair and turn your back, I will undress and wash. I have been longing to do that all day."

She had a feeling the Marquis's eyes were twinkling. But she told herself resolutely that they could both behave in a civilised and sensible manner. This was not the moment for prudery or flirtatious blushes.

They were fighting for their freedom, perhaps for their lives, and it was essential that both of them should sleep before they tackled the dangers which were waiting for them on the morrow.

The Marquis picked up the bucket.

"Shall I pour some water into the basin for you?" he asked.

"Yes please," Lucretia answered.

At that moment they heard Madame's heavy footsteps coming up the stairs.

Quickly the Marquis put down the bucket and sat down on the chair hunching his shoulders. There was a knock on the door.

"Come in," Lucretia said.

"I have brought you a taper," Madame Croix said. "It will be dark before you are in bed, and I also

158

thought as you had no luggage you might like to borrow a night-gown."

"How very kind you are!" Lucretia answered.

She took the taper and the gown from the French woman.

"*Bonsoir, Madame.*"

u"*Bonsoir, et merci bien!*" Lucretia replied.

The sabots clattered down the stairs, and Lucretia set the thin cheap taper down on the table.

Then she had done so she looked at the night-gown. She gave a little hastily repressed laugh and held it up.

"Look!" she cried, "I should be safe even with Casanova in a gown like this!"

Of heavy flannel it had been thickened and shrunk by many washes until the wool itself was heavy and unyielding. It had long sleeves and was buttoned right to the neck.

Lucretia held it against herself.

"I had thought," the Marquis said in an unsteady voice, "that I was so fatigued that even the proximity of the Venus de Milo would leave me unmoved tonight. But now I am not sure."

They were both suddenly seized with irrepressible laughter. For a moment it seemed as though the Marquis was unable to control his merriment, and Lucretia in alarm put her hand over his mouth.

As she did so he put his hand over hers and she felt his lips warm and insistent against her palm.

For a moment they were both very still. Then Lucretia snatched her hand away.

"Turn your back," she said sharply. "The sooner we rest the better."

As she undressed she felt so tired that she was hardly conscious of the Marquis sitting with his back to her.

She washed, finding that the cold water even without any soap removed a lot of the grime and dust of the miles they had walked.

Then she put on the heavy flannel night-gown and crossed the room to the bed.

"I will sleep nearest the wall," she said.

She got in feeling the feathers like a cloud beneath her, and pulling down one of the pillows she set it in the centre of the bed.

"I am going to wash very thoroughly," she heard the Marquis say, "so if your maidenly modesty will be offended, I suggest you keep your eyes shut."

"I will," Lucretia answered.

She heard him empty the basin of the water that she had used and fill it up again. Then a delicious feeling of languor seeped over her.

She was sinking ... sinking into a darkness that was the most comfortable thing she had ever known.

Lucretia felt herself coming back to consciousness by degrees through layer upon layer of sleep. Now she could hear the Marquis's heart beating and thought she must be in the wood.

She felt the same sense of security that she had known the night before.

He was there and nothing mattered, the danger was unimportant, they were together.

The wood was very comfortable, her legs were still aching, but they were resting and she was warm as she had not been warm the night before.

She was suddenly aware that she was lying close against the Marquis and he had his arm around her. She was curled up beside him, her cheek was against his heart and there was no pillow between them.

She was so sleepy that it did not seem to matter. She was warm, comfortable, and she loved him.

"I love you," she tried to whisper in her heart.

Then sleep took her away again and she seemed to sink lower and lower into the softness of the feather bed.

Lucretia woke with a jerk. Someone had his hand on her shoulder and was shaking it.

"Wake up, Lucretia, we have to be moving!"

She opened her eyes. The Marquis was standing beside the bed dressed in his tattered uniform.

160

"I am . . . so . . . sleepy," she murmured, her lips moving slowly.

"I know," he answered, "but it is five o'clock and we have to start at once if we are to reach the yacht before it is dark."

Lucretia gave a little sigh. It was almost an agony not to shut her eyes, not to drift back into the warm darkness.

"Lucretia!" the Marquis said sharply, and she sat up as if at the word of a command.

He smiled at her.

"I will go downstairs and see if there is any chance of breakfast," he said. "Hurry and get dressed."

"I will," she answered.

She felt as if in trying to go on sleeping she had behaved like a school girl. As soon as he had left the room, she jumped out of bed and hastily put on her clothes.

There was no time to do more than wash her hands and face, and then she adjusted her white cap, that was rather crumpled by now, in front of the mirror and decided from what she could see of herself that she made a very passable French woman.

She clattered down stairs in her clogs to find the Marquis seated at the breakfast table eating a boiled egg.

"There's an egg for each of you this morning!" Madame Croix said with a note of triumph in her voice. "I remembered a nest I didn't visit last night."

"You are too kind, Madame," Lucretia said, sitting down gratefully at the table and picking up a spoon.

"I am frying some bread for your man, I expect you would like some too."

"I would indeed!" Lucretia replied, thinking it was many years since she had eaten fried bread in the nursery.

The food was delicious. They gulped down the coffee and were ready to leave.

Madame Croix looking at the Marquis suddenly said: "One moment, I have an idea."

She went into another room and came back with a

161

large pair of boots. They were well worn, but they were a far bigger size than those the Marquis had on.

"These were my husband's," Madame said. "He will not need them again, but your man could do with them. He cannot walk far in those broken things."

"Are you sure you can spare them?" Lucretia asked.

"Who would need them but my younger boy?" Madame Croix asked. "But they are too big for him and he will have his brother's to choose from."

Again her voice was bitter, and Lucretia taking the boots said:

"Thank you ... There is nothing else I can say except thank you very much indeed."

She put them down beside the Marquis who sat down on a chair, and then as she saw him deliberately fumble rather slowly with the laces of the boots he had on, she knelt down beside him.

"I'll do it," she said.

She undid the laces with deft fingers and pulled the battered open-toed boot from his left foot.

As she did so she saw the blisters on his skin. They were large and must have been very painful.

Then as her hands touched him she lifted her face and looked up at him and their eyes met.

There was an expression in his face that she had never seen before and it held her spell-bound. They were very near to each other and somehow it was quite impossible to breathe.

For what seemed to Lucretia almost an eternity of time without words, their eyes spoke to each other and then with an inarticulate little murmur of her lips, she put the new boots on to the Marquis's feet and tied the laces.

He managed the other himself. Somehow she felt curiously weak as if she had passed through a strange emotional experience that she did not understand.

Lucretia rose to her feet.

"Please, *Madame*, you must let us pay you," she said, "in return for your kindness in having us here all night, for the food which has made all the difference,

162

and for these boots which will help my husband on his journey."

"I want nothing," Madame Croix said. "It has been a pleasure to have you, *Madame*, and that's the truth. As for your husband, he is in the hands of *le Bon Dieu*. I can only pray for him."

"But *Madame* . . ." Lucretia began to expostulate.

The Marquis touched her hand as if inadvertently and she understood. Somehow he had managed to leave Madame Croix money where she would find it later.

She walked up to the French woman.

"Please pray for us," she said, "we are both deeply in need of your prayers."

"I'll do that," the woman said.

On an impulse Lucretia bent forward and kissed the older woman's cheek.

"Je vous remercie," she said.

Then the Marquis bowed and shuffling his feet moved away.

It was a little while before they could walk normally and only then did she speak.

"You left her money?" Lucretia asked.

"Under my pillow," the Marquis replied, "as if I had put it there for safety and forgotten it."

"I am glad," Lucretia answered, "she was very kind."

She had a feeling they were both saying things to each other which could not be expressed in words.

But she knew too that the Marquis was anxious and apprehensive of what lay ahead.

For today, when they neared the sea, they would be in the greatest danger of being caught.

CHAPTER 9

Lucretia changed the clogs for her own shoes, and the Marquis hung them over his shoulder as he had done before.

As he did so he glanced round the countryside, and she had the feeling that he was more alert than he had been the previous day for the sight of a soldier or of anyone who might try to talk to them.

They set off at a good pace travelling over open fields, but Lucretia noticed that after they had gone a mile or so the land became less flat, and there were clumps of trees and an occasional small wood which gave her a feeling of confidence.

Feeling it was important to keep cheerful she chattered away to the Marquis, talking about his neighbours at Merlyncourt or telling him of the swans that had been nesting earlier in the year in the vicinity of the Dower House.

He appeared interested, but she knew that at the same time one part of his mind was concerned with the danger which faced them ahead and the difficulty of reaching the yacht without being apprehended.

"Do you think the French are still looking for us?" Lucretia asked after a little while.

She thought it was a mistake to dwell upon their precarious situation and yet it was impossible not to ask the question.

"If Lord Beaumont has reached the yacht, as I hope he has," the Marquis answered, "then they may connect us with his escape. On the other hand they will

164

undoubtedly think our behaviour somewhat suspicious, especially as you laid out two of their company!"

He smiled and added:

"It is something of which neither the officer nor the soldier who was guarding me will be particularly proud. No man likes to be vanquished by a woman, especially one as small and slight as you!"

"Perhaps they will think I was a man in disguise," Lucretia suggested.

"There is little chance of that," the Marquis answered looking at her large eyes and the slim fragility of her whole appearance.

Even in the peasant-dress that was too big for her she made other women seem in comparison large and clumsy.

What was more she moved with a grace that was instinctive, but which could not easily be associated with someone who could stun a man with a bottle.

"Perhaps they will think they dreamt the whole episode," he said suddenly.

She looked up at him in surprise.

"Why should they do that?"

"Because you look like someone out of a dream."

Her eyes widened and, realising from the tone of his voice that it was a compliment, instinctively something within her leapt with a strange excitement.

He had never said anything like this to her before, and she knew that it meant more than a conventional appreciation of her appearance or even after their marriage his telling her that she had looked lovely.

It was hard to know what to reply. In fact it was obvious that the Marquis was not expecting an answer, because now he was looking towards the horizon and frowning.

"There is bad weather ahead!"

Lucretia followed the direction of his eyes. The sky above them was overcast and in the West was dark and ominous as if a storm was brewing.

"Does that mean that the yacht will find it hard to find an anchorage?" she enquired.

"It means that for protection it will have to come in

close to the cliffs," the Marquis replied, "and therefore it may be sighted."

Then he shrugged his shoulders.

"Perhaps I am being unduly apprehensive! It is just that I wish to get you away safely from this accursed soil."

"Do you really hate the French?" Lucretia asked, thinking of Madame Croix and how kind she had been to them.

As if the Marquis read her thoughts he answered:

"Not the French peasants, who have little idea of what is happening. But I loathe and detest Bonaparte for the misery and suffering he has caused all over Europe, for the thousands of men who lie dead or maimed as a sop to his ambition.

"War has its moments of glory, Lucretia, but make no mistake, the end is always the same, devastation and desolation for the innocent!"

"Now you understand what I felt when I visited the hospital in Paris," she answered. "But I could not hate the wounded men because they were French. I felt in a way that they belonged to no nationality but were just puppets for those who pulled the strings."

"A French puppet can still kill an Englishman," the Marquis answered grimly.

She knew he was thinking of his comrades who had fallen beside him in battle.

They walked on covering over three miles, and now there were more hamlets and small villages which they skirted, more people working in the fields and occasionally they saw in the distance a cart or a coach travelling along a road.

The Marquis's pace kept increasing and Lucretia found it hard to keep up with him.

Then as they were crossing a narrow country road, passing from one field to another, round the corner came a farm-cart driven at a spanking pace by a young man wearing the traditional peasants smock, but with his hat at an angle and a red poppy stuck in the hat-band.

There was no time to hide or even to cross the road.

166

The Marquis hunched himself up and they stood still waiting for the cart to pass them. The young farmer drew his horse to a standstill.

"Where are you going?" he asked. "Your man doesn't appear to be in very good shape."

He looked at the bandage round the Marquis's head as he spoke.

"My husband has been wounded, *Monsieur*," Lucretia replied, "and we are travelling to Les Pieux."

The young farmer let out a whistle.

"That's quite some way," he said, "but I can take you a few miles of your journey. I'm going to the market in Le Vretot."

"That is very kind," Lucretia said, "but . . ."

She glanced uncertainly at the Marquis as she spoke and saw him give an almost imperceptible nod of his head and went on:

"If it is no trouble, *merci bien, Monsieur*, we would be very grateful."

"Then get your man into the cart," the young farmer said, "and you can come up beside me."

He did not get down to assist, which seemed surprising. Lucretia made a pretence of helping the Marquis to climb into the back of the high-sided cart which was empty.

Then after taking the opportunity of slipping on her clogs and hiding her own shoes in the pocket of her big apron she climbed up beside the young farmer.

As she did so she saw that he had a wooden stump instead of a left leg.

"You have been injured!" she exclaimed.

"A cannon ball got me," he answered. "It was good luck as it happened because it meant I could get back to my farm."

He was a man, she decided, of about twenty-five, red faced and jolly and looked surprisingly well fed.

His horse too was in fine fettle, and Lucretia felt that he must be one of the more prosperous farmers.

The Frenchman glanced over his shoulder to see if the Marquis who was huddled down with his back to

167

them in the cart was all right, and whipped up his horse.

"It is quite a step to Les Pieux," he said. "Do you think your husband will make it?"

"He is very tired," Lucretia answered, "because he was shot in the head and was ill for a long time. But we shall get there—especially when we have someone as kind as you to give us a helping hand."

The young Frenchman gave her a glance out of the corner of his eyes.

"My name is Henri Lechamp," he said. "My father owns a lot of land round here."

Lucretia smiled.

"I thought you appeared prosperous, and you have a good horse."

"We have got some better ones up at the farm," Henri Lechamp boasted. "I'd like to show them to you."

"Perhaps I shall have the chance of seeing them one day," Lucretia said lightly, "but I would not wish to do this walk a second time."

"Perhaps I will be able to come over and fetch you," he suggested.

She realised there was a flirtatious look in his eyes.

"I expect you have a lot of hard work to do, Monsieur," she replied, "and I am sure like every other farmer in France you are short-handed."

"We are indeed!" Henri Lechamp replied. "But being the boss's son I get time off when I want it. I would like to see you again, *Madame*."

He paused and asked:

"What is your name?"

"Madame Deauvais," Lucretia answered. "My husband's parents live at Les Pieux which is why we are going there, so that he can rest and get well."

"Good luck to him!" Henri Lechamp said.

Then in a low voice he added out of the corner of his mouth:

"Are you fond of your husband?"

"Yes, very fond," Lucretia answered. "And I am very worried about him as you can imagine."

168

"A shot in the head is very bad," Henri Lechamp said. "I've seen men go raving mad after a bullet had but grazed their forehead or their scalp. Supposing he never gets better?"

"Oh he will!" Lucretia answered. "The doctors say it is only a temporary disability. All he wants is rest and quiet, and he will soon be himself."

"He looks a bit stupid to me," Henri Lechamp said.

"Well he cannot speak at the moment," Lucretia replied, "but he understands what is going on."

"Will he understand if you and I have a bit of fun together?" Henri Lechamp asked still in a low voice.

"He would indeed!" Lucretia answered warningly. "A man tried to touch me the other day and he very nearly killed him. He is very strong and he can be ferocious when he's aroused."

Henri Lechamp looked sulky and concentrated for a little while on the road ahead, and then he said, still in a low voice:

"We ought to be able to contrive something, you and I."

Lucretia could not help being amused. He was obviously the Don Juan of the neigbhorhood and had all the girls running after him. He did not contemplate for one moment that his advances would not be reciprocated.

"I am afraid it would be much too difficult," she said firmly.

"I expect I shall be able to make you change your mind," he answered.

She did not reply and after a moment he said:

"What part of the country do you come from? You are far too pretty to belong to Brittany. We're big fellows here and the girls find us handsome enough, but they're not much to look at themselves, as I found when I went to Paris."

"When were you in Paris?" Lucretia asked hoping to draw his attention from herself.

He launched into a long story of how he had been there for several months while he was in training with his Regiment.

He described somewhat lewdly all the fun he had enjoyed with a large number of young women.

As he talked Lucretia watched the road and realised they were drawing near to a village where she imagined the market would be taking place.

She guessed by the sun that it must be past midday, and she wondered how she could contrive to get Henri Lechamp to buy them some food.

"It is very kind of you to take us so far," she said interrupting his discourse about his conquests of the fair sex, "but I wonder if I would be imposing on your kindness if I asked you to buy us some bread and perhaps one of the delicious Camembert cheeses when we reach the market-place."

She looked at him and added quickly:

"We can pay for what we have."

"Of course I will get you anything you want," Henri Lechamp said obligingly. "And there's lots of other things I would like to give you, if you'd give me the chance."

As the village was almost in sight, Lucretia allowed herself to smile beguilingly at him.

"We have to get to Les Pieux," she said. "Perhaps one day I shall come back, who knows?"

"I will be waiting," he said, "that is if you don't see me turn up in Les Pieux first. You need not bother to give me your address, I'll just ask for the prettiest girl in the neighborhood."

"Married woman," Lucretia corrected.

"I don't mind telling you I think you are wasting your time with him," Henri Lechamp said jerking his head back towards the Marquis. "Why don't you and I enjoy ourselves? I can teach you more about *l'amour* than he's ever thought of."

"It is time you found a wife of your own," Lucretia answered. "There must be plenty of girls longing to marry you."

"You bet there are!" Henri Lechamp agreed. "And they would like to marry my father's fat acres! I am not taking one that doesn't bring me a big dowry.

170

That's more important than a pretty face when it comes to marriage."

"I am sure you are very sensible," Lucretia remarked surpressing an inclination to laugh.

They had reached the village by now and Lucretia saw the market was in progress. There were a number of small stalls and selling their wares there were women dressed like she was herself in red camlet jackets, high aprons, white caps with flying lappets, and wooden sabots.

There were eggs, butter, cheeses, live hens and vegetables for sale, all of which the women would have carried on their backs from the outlying neighbourhoods, starting early on the long trek when it was still dark.

"Why have you not anything to sell?" Lucretia asked as Henri Lechamp slowed the horse to move through the crowd wandering aimlessly around the square.

"I have come to buy!" he answered, "and with plenty of money in my pocket. There are ways and means, even in war time, for turning over a franc or two."

"I am glad to hear it," Lucretia said a little dryly. "I have seen so much poverty in France."

"Fools remain poor," Henri Lechamp said, "it's the clever ones that get rich. And that's me!"

"I'm sure you are very clever," Lucretia said.

He drew the horse to a standstill at the side of the market.

"Will you hold the reins while I go and see what I can find you?" he said. "He's a young horse, I can't leave him."

"Yes of course," Lucretia smiled.

"Have you handled a horse before?" Henri Lechamp asked.

"A lot of them," Lucretia replied, "you need not worry. I will keep him under control."

"I'll not be long," Henri Lechamp told her. "I'll get you what you want, bread, cheese, butter wasn't it? And then I'll attend to my own business."

Lucretia had the feeling by the way he said it that

171

his business, whatever it might be, was something rather shady. He clambered down the high side of the cart with great dexterity, his wooden leg apparently giving him very little trouble.

Standing up he was taller than she had expected and she saw by the way that his hair curled over his head and by the roving look in his eye that there was no doubt that he would strut about the market like a resplendent young cock in a farmyard.

As soon as he reached the ground Henri Lechamp was calling out and waving to acquaintances.

Then he crossed towards the stalls and she saw him going to where a woman was selling long crisp loaves of French bread. They looked so fresh and delicious, that Lucretia could almost feel her teeth crunching into them.

The only men in the market were a few very ancient ones, or small boys who were making a nuisance of themselves running and tumbling with each other in the dust and being continually shouted at by their elders.

There was a pen of goats who were all bleating piteously as if for their young, and in another pen there were a number of sheep waiting for purchasers.

It was all noisy and colourful and countrified. Lucretia was watching the people with interest, when suddenly she heard the Marquis say behind her:

"Drive on!"

She turned her head thinking she must be mistaken, and then without moving, still hunched down in the cart, he said sharply:

"Do as I say, drive on quickly!"

She opened her lips to argue and then saw what the Marquis had just seen, several soldiers moving through the crowds with a purposeful air about them.

Quickly she lifted the reins, touched the horse with a whip and instantly they were off again moving so quickly that people hustled their children out of the way and shouted after them as they passed.

Lucretia thought that she heard Henri Lechamp's voice shouting too, but she did not look back.

172

"Keep on," the Marquis ordered.

The village was a small one and in a few seconds they had passed the last house and were out of sight of the market.

It was then that the Marquis, getting up from the back of the cart, clambered to the front and took the reins from Lucretia.

He brought the whip down on the horse's back and sprang it into a gallop, so that the wooden cart rattled and creaked and bounced down the road. But they were moving at a pace that Lucretia knew anyone would find hard to overtake.

"Were they the soldiers who alerted you?" she asked.

"They were looking for deserters," the Marquis said. "I might have known they would be in every market."

"But they would have thought you were wounded."

"I should still have been questioned," the Marquis replied, "and I have, as you well know, no papers."

"Poor Monsieur Lechamp, I feel we have treated him very badly in taking away his cart and horse," Lucretia said.

"Lecherous young swine!" the Marquis remarked violently. "He deserves all he gets!"

Lucretia smiled.

"Are you not somewhat ungrateful? He had gone to buy us our luncheon."

"I heard your conversation," the Marquis said. "On a journey such as this, your face is not your fortune, Lucretia, it is a damned nuisance."

"You are very complimentary," Lucretia laughed.

It was difficult to talk because the Marquis was driving so quickly.

He kept looking back over his shoulder, and though it was hard to see through the cloud of dust they were leaving behind them, it appeared that no-one was following them.

"We can thank God that the military are not mounted in this part of the country," the Marquis said. "And what is more, there are very few horses left. Bonaparte wants them all for the war."

"Are we going to drive all the way to Les Pieux?" Lucretia asked.

"No, not too far," the Marquis said, "that could be dangerous. If Lechamp tells those who are interested that we said we were going to Le Pieux, it is the last place they would now expect us to go to."

"I see your reasoning," Lucretia said.

They drove on for perhaps three miles, and then the road turned sharply to the South. The Marquis drew the horse to a standstill.

"I want you to jump out of the cart," he said, "without leaving any trace of your footsteps on the road. Can you manage that?"

"Of course," Lucretia answered seeing there was a green grass edging to what was little more than a narrow cartway.

"Very well," the Marquis said, "jump when you are ready."

She did as he told her, landing safely on the grass verge.

The Marquis knotted the reins onto the dash-board, then followed her onto the grass.

He gave the horse a touch of the whip and as it moved off sharply down the road, he threw the whip into the back of the cart.

Lucretia looked at the wheel-tracks on the soft road and realised why he had taken such measures.

"They will follow the cart!" she said.

"That is the idea," the Marquis agreed, "and now we are back to walking again. You had better put on your own shoes and give me your clogs."

She did as she was told and they took to the fields.

"It is a pity we could not have waited to run away until after luncheon," Lucretia said. "It sounds incredibly greedy, but I am beginning to be hungry again."

"I am sorry for you," the Marquis answered, "but at the same time I was a fool to go into the village. I might have guessed it would be dangerous."

"You could not anticipate the soldiers would be there."

174

"They are everywhere," he said harshly, "and that is something I should have remembered. Bonaparte is desperate for men. He is calling up boys of seventeen. He is taking into the Army any man, however decrepit, who can hold a musket."

"Why did he break the peace?" Lucretia asked. "Had he not gained enough? The whole of Europe belongs to him!"

"But not England!" the Marquis said quietly. "He will never rest until he has defeated us and that he will never do."

"I hope . . . not," Lucretia said a little uncertainly.

The Marquis was walking very quickly and she found it easier not to talk. She realised he wanted to get as far away as possible from Le Vretot.

At the same time she thought it was a pity they could not have gone even further in the cart.

Her soles were very sore and she could not bear to think of the blisters on the Marquis's feet and how he must be suffering. However she consoled herself that his new boots must be much more comfortable than the ones he had been wearing.

They walked on and on, and now Lucretia's hunger was as it had been the day before, like a hole in her stomach.

She began to think of all the succulent things she had eaten in the past and how little she had appreciated them.

The fried bread she had for breakfast had been more delectable than the quails in aspic she had eaten at grand dinners, or the delicately cooked veal with mushrooms which was one of her father's favourite dishes, or the great Boar's Head that was prepared by their chef at Christmas as a special treat.

"And if I am hungry," she thought to herself, "how much worse it must be for the Marquis! He is so big and strong and he needs good food to sustain him."

They found a spring and quenched their thirst, but the Marquis would not linger and they walked on again keeping now to the shelter of woods whenever it was possible and avoiding open ground or roads.

The sky was growing steadily darker and suddenly there was a scud of rain carried on a wind that Lucretia could only hope came from the sea.

She asked herself if there was a taste of salt in the air, but could not be certain of it.

Surely they must have come a very long way and Les Pieux could not be much further.

But she would not speak of it to the Marquis, thinking how annoying she would find it if she herself was trying to find the way and someone kept asking idiotic questions.

On and on they went plodding over heavy ground, finding that where there had been dust it was now turning to mud as the rain had began to fall incessantly.

"I would give you my coat," the Marquis said, "but I feel I would look rather suspicious in my shirt sleeves."

"Do not be so ridiculous!" Lucretia replied. "As it happens, this jacket is very thick, but if the rain gets worse it will go through everything—your coat as well as mine."

"The one cheering thing about it," the Marquis said, "is that the French are not fond of rain. A French soldier will avoid it at all costs."

"Let us hope you are right," Lucretia answered.

They passed through a wood which was on the side of a hill and they reached the top moving with difficulty through the low branches, before finding the trees sloped down to a valley below.

It was when they were almost emerging from the wood to cross into open country that the Marquis looking up the road saw some soldiers approaching.

Quickly he drew Lucretia back into the shadow of the trees and then as the men grew nearer he dragged her into some bushes and they crouched down out of sight.

It was a squad of four men in charge of a Corporal, but it was enough to make Lucretia tremble and slip her hand into the Marquis's.

She felt him almost crush her fingers in his, and as the soldiers drew nearer she held her breath.

However they were obviously not reconnoitring or

looking for strangers, but were marching sharply through the rain to some unknown destination. The Marquis drew a sigh of relief.

"They have gone," Lucretia said.

"There will be others," he answered. "I warned you that as we neared the coast the French would be on their guard."

They walked for another two miles before having climbed a small hill they saw far away in the distance the sea meeting the horizon.

Lucretia turned towards the Marquis with a light in her eyes.

"We have done it!" she cried. "We have reached the sea!"

"Not yet," the Marquis said, but although his tone was cautious she knew by the expression on his face that he too was pleased.

"We must be careful, very careful," he said, "and from now on keep only to the woods."

There were not many of them and they had to zig-zag across the countryside, going from one clump of trees to another.

But all the time they were getting nearer and nearer to the sea and Lucretia felt her hopes rising.

The ground was difficult to walk over. First it was sandy in which their feet sank so that every footstep was an effort, and then rough and stony which as the soles of her shoes were thin was very painful.

The clouds seemed to get lower, the sky got darker and more ominous overhead, and now the rain which had been persistent but not too cold was almost torrential.

Lucretia was soaked to the skin. She could feel rivulets of rain running over her whole body and she knew the Marquis must be the same.

It became more and more difficult to see as the rain beat against them, and at times they walked almost blindly, their eyes half shut against the violence of it.

The Marquis took Lucretia by the hand so that they should not get separated, and as they dodged from copse to copse and sometimes from tree to tree, she thought that he was taking unnecessary precautions.

It would be hard for anyone, even searching the country side with a spy-glass, to see anything but rain sheeting down grey and relentless.

After a time Lucretia began to find it hard even to think. All she was conscious of was the necessity to put one foot in front of the other.

Left foot—right foot—left foot—right foot! It seemed at times as if her brain could hardly force her feet to obey her will.

She was very cold and now the rain water running down her back and over her breasts felt like icy streaks pouring down from a snow-peaked mountain.

Her petticoats were clinging to her legs. A gust of wind blew away her white cap, and because the Marquis did not notice it she felt it was too much effort to go back and pick it up.

They were having to force themselves forward against the whole force of the wind, some gusts seemed to keep them standing still so that it was impossible to move.

Left foot—right foot—left foot—right foot!

Lucretia felt it was a sheer impossibility to move any further. It was like pushing against a wall of water, the rain hurt her face with its violence and her hands no longer seemed to belong to her.

She began to lag behind and the Marquis dragged her forward as if to force her to keep up with him.

Her foot caught a stone and with a little cry she fell down, knowing as she did so that it would be impossible ever to get up again.

As she lay there cold and drenched, past thought and past speech, she felt him lift her up into his arms.

She put her face against his shoulder.

"I am . . . sorry," she tried to say, "I . . . I will be all . . . right in a moment . . . " but somehow the words sounded jumbled even to herself.

"Keep still!" the Marquis said and his arms tightened round her.

With an effort Lucretia put out her arm and put it

178

round his neck. Vaguely she remembered someone telling her it was easier to carry a person that way.

Her mind had gone far, far away from her, lost down a long tunnel. She could not think any longer.

"I will go on walking," she wanted to tell the Marquis, but the words would not come.

Instead she was conscious only that she did not have to move her feet and that he was holding her very close.

"I ought to hear his heart beating," she thought.

Then with her face hidden against him so that the rain was no longer hurting her skin, she knew no more.

Lucretia opened her eyes very slowly. For a moment she could not think where she was. There was a low ceiling, the white painted walls were somehow familiar and yet for a moment she could not place them.

Then she realised she was in a bed and she realised that she was in the yacht.

She closed her eyes, feeling it must be a dream. Then as she opened them again she saw as she turned her head the clock beside her bed. The hands pointed to half after noon.

"It could not be possible!" she thought. She could not have been there asleep for so long.

The curtains were drawn over the portholes, but the sun was peeping through them and she could see two white towels lying on the floor near the bed and beyond them, in a heap in the corner of the cabin, her sodden red camlet jacket and cotton petticoats.

She was safe! They had made it! They had reached the yacht!

For a moment she was too tired to think, too tired even to feel elated. Then she opened her eyes again to be quite certain she had not been mistaken.

No, there were the expensive fittings and comfortable accoutrements of the Marquis's yacht, and he had brought her to it in safety.

She tried to remember what had happened, but she could only recall the rain beating down, the moment she had fallen, and his picking her up in his arms! Everything else was a blank.

How could she have been unconscious or asleep during the last part of their journey?

She tried to reconstruct what had happened. He must have carried her to the cliff side and climbing down must have been precarious. But he had managed it and in the place appointed, he had found the boat with its British sailors waiting to carry them back to the yacht.

How could she have been unconscious through all that? How could she not have known that they had won through and succeeded against almost desperate odds in evading the French?

It had been a brilliant effort on the part of the Marquis to move right across enemy territory, to evade recapture, and to sail back to England without mishap.

"We must be in port now," Lucretia thought, "because the yacht is still and there is no sound of lapping waves."

She wondered where they were and yet felt too limp to move and find out.

She was still half asleep and then as her brain became clearer she found herself remembering all too vividly—the way they had escaped from the market-place in the cart, the moment when they had hidden in the woods to watch the soldiers march by, and those last terrifying and exhausting miles with the rain beating down upon them.

And yet, Lucretia thought, perhaps it had been a blessing in disguise.

The French guarding the cliffs would undoubtedly have taken shelter, thus making it easier for the Marquis to slip past them and reach the waiting boat.

"I am home! Safe and back in England!"

And then suddenly Lucretia remembered that it was also the end of the adventure.

She felt an irrepressible urgency to find out what had happened. She pushed back the bed clothes and as she did so she realised she was naked!

For a moment she was very still. There was only one person who could have undressed her, dried her and put her to bed!

She pushed aside the bed clothes, rose a little unsteadily to her feet and walked across the cabin to the porthole to push back the curtains.

Yes, they were in harbour and she imagined it was Poole from where they had set out.

She stood looking out for a moment and then she shut the curtains again. She did not want to look. She did not wish to see the familiarity of English soil.

Going to the chest which stood in the corner of the room she pulled out a night-gown and put it on. Then she found a chiffon wrap, threw it around her shoulders and moved back towards the bed.

She had meant to ring the bell, but as she put out her hand towards it there came a knock on the door.

Lucretia slipped under the bed clothes and lying against the pillows said a little nervously:

"Come in."

She had hoped it might be the Marquis, but instead it was the Chief steward, a man called Jarvis who had been in the service of the Marquis for many years.

"Good morning, M'Lady," he said, "I heard you moving and I had His Lordship's instructions to bring you some food the moment you woke."

"Is His Lordship all right?" Lucretia asked.

"As happy as a sandboy, if I may use the expression, M'Lady!" Jarvis answered. "His Lordship slept like a log for twelve hours."

He put the tray he was carrying down beside the bed.

"Some nourishing soup, M'Lady, just what His Lordship takes himself after one of these 'ere escapades of his. And a chicken omelette. His Lordship ordered it special for you and he hoped also you would take a glass of wine."

"Where is His Lordship?" Lucretia had to ask the question.

"He's ashore, M'Lady, with Lord Beaumont and the young gentleman. They were in a hurry to get back to

London to see the Prince of Wales, and His Lordship has gone with them to make arrangements for their journey."

"The boat picked them up in St. Pierre Bay?"

"Yes, indeed, M'Lady, and they told us how His Lordship and yourself had been apprehended by the soldiers. Very worried and anxious we've been! But we need not have troubled ourselves, His Lordship's always the same! He outwits them Frenchies every time! He is too clever for 'em and that's a fact."

Lucretia was listening to him wide-eyed and he said in the kindly tone of a nurse to a small child:

"Now come along, M'Lady, drink your soup while its hot."

Lucretia did as she was told and felt that it gave her a little more strength.

As she ate the omelette and drank the glass of wine that was on the tray, the Steward started to collect her wet clothes and towels from the floor of the cabin.

"Now, M'Lady," Jarvis said, "His Lordship wants you to rest until dinner-time, when he hopes your Ladyship will do him the honour of dining with him."

"He does not want to see me before that?" Lucretia asked.

"I think not, M'Lady. As soon as His Lordship returns we are going to move a short way down the coast to somewhere special. His Lordship will want to tell you about it himself."

Jarvis picked up the tray.

"And, M'Lady, if you will take my advice, you'll rest while you can. His Lordship's as strong as a horse. He'll come back to us dead beat, and after a good sleep is ready to enjoy himself again. But Your Ladyship's not as strong as he is, and who'd expect you to be?"

He smiled at her in a kind paternal fashion and going from the cabin shut the door.

Lucretia turned her face against the pillows, then quite suddenly she began to cry!

CHAPTER 10

"I have failed!" Lucretia sobbed.

She felt that the Marquis had won a great victory in getting them home safely, while she personally had been utterly and ignominiously defeated.

She had believed during those two days and two nights when they had been together—which seemed now like a whole life-time—that somehow she would win him to her, and that she would discover that he loved her at least a little.

But she had lost the battle, and now there was nothing left but darkness, misery and the utter loneliness of the future.

She felt as if not only was she outside the gates of Merlyncourt, but there was no chance of her ever going through them.

As she sobbed she bitterly regretted that she had not let the Marquis stay with her the night they were married.

He had said that before she "made love, a man must love her body, her heart, and her soul." That was indeed how she loved him, but he would never, she thought despairingly, feel the same for her.

Yet if she had become his wife without love she would at least have had the wonder and thrill of feeling his mouth on hers, his hands touching her!

"But he is not even interested in my body," Lucretia told herself miserably.

He had undressed her last night, taken off her wet clothes, dried her and put her into bed, and it had meant nothing to him!

"Had he kissed me," she thought, "it would have awakened me even if I were dead!"

No! In his mind she obviously was of no consequence! She was just an encumberance—a woman in whom he had no interest, not even a physical one!

"Yet I love him . . . I love him . . . I love him!" Lucretia cried in an aching agony of unhappiness.

The only memory she had left of their mock marriage was when he placed his mouth on hers to prevent her speaking, and one strange incredible moment when kneeling at his feet she had looked up into his eyes and had seen there an expression which stirred her to the very depths of her being.

Yet she must have been mistaken in thinking it significant! She had failed, she had lost him!

Lucretia's tears became a tempest which shook her whole body, she cried until she could cry no more, and then because she was utterly exhausted, she slept.

Lucretia was woken by Jarvis coming into the cabin to prepare her bath.

"I'm sorry to wake you, M'Lady," he said, "but 'tis seven o'clock."

Lucretia sat up.

"Seven o'clock!" she exclaimed, "it cannot be as late as that!"

"It is, M'Lady, but His Lordship didn't wish you to be disturbed."

Lucretia looked at her clock as if she could not believe that Jarvis was telling her the truth. She must have slept for nearly seven hours, and she knew that, while she was still depressed, she felt better in herself and was not tired.

When Jarvis had left the room she got out of bed and walked to her mirror. When she saw her reflection she gave an exclamation of horror!

There were dark lines under her eyes, and it was a very woebegone, unhappy face which stared back at her.

She washed her tears away first in hot water then in cold, and covered her eye-lids with witch hazel before she bathed in the warm flower-scented bath and felt the last remnants of fatigue ebbing away from her.

She had thought it would be a waste of time to use the cosmetics which Mr. Odrowski had chosen.

"It is unlikely the Marquis will notice how I look," she told herself miserably.

As Jarvis had said, he was now ready "to enjoy himself again," and that meant he would be thinking of meeting Lady Hester. That would be the last humiliation!

Even so she could not allow him to guess how unhappy she was. So very carefully Lucretia used the lotions and salves with which she had been supplied.

She made her eyes look mysterious, but she knew, even as she did so, there was no longer any glint in them. In fact she had lost hope.

When she was ready for her gown, she opened the big cupboard which had been built along one wall of the cabin and saw the glittering array of glamorous dresses which had been specially designed for her performance as an experienced and sophisticated woman of the world.

Somehow she could not bear to look at them or to contemplate wearing them. They, like her pretended sophistication was the weapon which had not saved her from defeat. Instead she chose a very plain robe of deep blue gauze which matched the colour of her eyes.

It was almost Grecian in shape and had been designed to wear with some magnificent sapphires which had belonged to her mother. But Lucretia did not open her jewel-case.

She had a violent distaste this evening for decking herself out or for striving in any manner to draw attention to her looks.

She did not even arrange her hair in the style which Mr. Odrowski had suggested to make her look older and more alluring.

Instead she parted it in the middle and merely coiled it at the base of her neck. Then, picking up a wide blue scarf which matched her dress, she threw it over her shoulders and walked from the cabin to the Saloon.

The Marquis was waiting for her, and as she came through the door Lucretia, despite her depression, felt her heart turn a somersault within her breast.

She had forgotten how handsome, how elegant he was. With his high snowy-white cravat, frilled shirt and perfectly fitting evening clothes, he looked very different from the man who yesterday had walked beside her in the tattered dirty uniform of a French soldier.

Their eyes met across the Saloon and for a moment neither of them spoke.

Lucretia did not realise that in the deep blue gown she had chosen, with her hair drawn back from her oval forehead, she looked more than ever the living embodiment of the early Italian Madonnas with whom the Marquis had identified her when he had come to her bedroom on their wedding night.

"You are rested?"

His voice was very deep and made her quiver as she moved slowly towards him.

"I am . . . ashamed to have slept for so . . . long."

He smiled at her and she suddenly felt as if the sun had come out!

"If you are as hungry as I am, we had best go ashore."

"Ashore?" she questioned.

"Come and look," he suggested.

She preceded him up the companion-way, and when she stood on deck she gave a little gasp of astonishment.

When she had risen to have her bath, she had realised the yacht was no longer moving, but she was too unhappy even to be curious.

Now she saw they were anchored in a tiny harbour, so small it was little more than a cove, and the gangplank led onto a narrow stone jetty. All around them growing down the side of the cliff in endless profusion, were azaleas and rhododendrons.

Their blossoms, crimson, yellow, red, white and pink, were breathtaking, and so was their fragrance which seemed to be mixed with the salty tang of the sea.

Raising her eyes, Lucretia could see a house, high on the cliffs and standing back a little way from the harbour. It looked, she thought, not unlike a Grecian temple with white pillars gleaming in the last remnants of the evening sunshine.

"Who lives here?" she asked.

"I do," the Marquis replied.

She looked up at him in surprise and he added:

"It is my secret hideaway."

Lucretia knew then without being told that this was where he stayed when he was on one of his dangerous missions to France.

Here was a safe harbour for his yacht, from which he could slip across the Channel without being perceived by the French ships which watched the more normal routes.

As if he knew she understood, the Marquis said no more but led her up a long flight of stone steps. They moved between shrubs and flowers over which bees buzzed and butterflies in a dozen different colours hovered.

They climbed higher and higher until Lucretia saw that the house was larger than she had thought and very beautiful.

Behind the pillars there was a loggia from which there obviously was a magnificent view of the sea. There were lilies growing in large bronze pots and jasmine in golden profusion.

The Marquis led Lucretia into a cool Hall exquisitely furnished, and from there into an oval Dining-Room where there was a table laid for dinner and lit by candles in a silver candelabra.

"Jarvis told me that you ate a very small luncheon," the Marquis said. "We have a lot of meals to make up for—you and I."

Course succeeded course and they were waited on, Lucretia noticed, by Jarvis and the other steward from the yacht.

She was hungry at first, but soon the acuteness of her hunger passed and she could savour the delicious

187

sauces and appreciate the dainty manner in which every dish was decorated.

"You have a superlative Chef!" she said.

The Marquis laughed.

"Dare I tell you 'he' is a woman and she is French!"

"French!" Lucretia exclaimed.

"Married to an Englishman," he explained. "I brought Newman and his wife over from France on one of my first expeditions. They were lucky to get away because Newman was to have been interned. They look after the house when I am not here, and when I am, as you can see, they spoil me with cooking that usually one can get only on the other side of the Channel."

The Marquis's eyes twinkled and he said:

"I will be honest and tell you that I also brought home the wine you are drinking without paying duty on it, you must admit it is very fine."

"I think if you are not careful you will be arrested for smuggling," Lucretia warned him in mock alarm.

"In which case," the Marquis replied, "I am certain you will save me from swinging from the gallows at Tyburn."

Lucretia did not answer, and soon as the Marquis went on talking she realised that he was deliberately contriving to entertain and amuse her.

He told her of some of the ways in which he had outwitted the French and arranged the escape of dozens of Englishmen and women without being caught.

He described to her his disguises. She was incredulous at his cleverness as he assumed a French dialect, or by merely altering the expression on his face appeared to become the humble clerk, the self-important industrialist or a petty bourgeois.

She had never known him so animated. She had never before known him look so young or so gay.

When finally the stewards withdrew from the Dining-room leaving only four candles on the table alight, the Marquis sat back in his chair with a glass of brandy in his hand.

He had insisted that Lucretia should drink a little

of a French liqueur which he told her had been made by monks and which he had also brought over in his yacht.

"Lord Beaumont must have been very glad to reach England in safety," Lucretia said.

"He was profuse in his gratitude," the Marquis replied. "And I know the Prime Minister will be pleased. He wanted him home."

There was silence for a moment and then Lucretia said hesitatingly:

"Will you . . . have to go . . . back to collect other . . . people?"

She felt as she asked the question that she could not bear to think of his going into danger alone, and yet she knew that, however much she pleaded, he would never take her with him.

"How can I endure it?" she asked herself. "To remain at home . . . to know that every second there is the likelihood of his being captured and taken to Paris before the Tribunal and perhaps . . . shot?"

The Marquis took a sip of his brandy before he replied:

"I think it is unlikely that my services will be required to rescue many more prisoners. Lord Beaumont tells me that the opportunities of escape are now practically non-existent. The French dislike being made to look fools and last year I did, as a matter of fact, make them look very foolish."

"So no more will get away?" Lucretia said with an eagerness she could not suppress.

The Marquis shook his head.

"No, poor devils! They will have to stay in enemy hands until the end of the war. Lord Beaumont tells me that the more distinguished prisioners are being moved from Paris further south to Avignon or Lyon."

"I am glad," Lucretia said involuntarily.

The Marquis looked at her and for a moment it seemed as if he would say something. Instead he rose to his feet.

"I want to show you the sunset," he said, "it is very beautiful."

189

He led the way from the Dining-Room and then drew Lucretia up an oak staircase to the first floor.

He opened a door and she walked into a room which she saw at a glance had an unsurpassed and quite incredible view of the sea.

There were six windows built in a semi-circle. Already the sun was sinking and the sky crimson and gold was reflected on the smooth surface of the water.

"What a wonderful room!" Lucretia exclaimed.

"I am glad you should think so," the Marquis answered. "I designed it myself so that when I lie here I can almost feel that I am at sea in some great galleon."

Lucretia turned her head as he spoke and realised that this was not, as she had thought, a Saloon but a bed-room.

There was an enormous four-poster, gilded and decorated with carvings of dolphins and other sea-creatures.

She stared at it in surprise, thinking it was the strangest and yet one of the most beautiful beds she had ever seen.

"My grandfather purchased it in Italy," the Marquis explained. "I thought it was eminently suitable for this house, so I transported it here from Merlyncourt."

"It is fantastic," Lucretia murmured, looking at the crimson silk hangings which were embroidered with the Merlyn Coat-of-Arms.

Then she saw that the bed was turned back and lying on it was one of her own night-gowns.

"If we are staying here tonight," she said quickly. "I must not turn you out of your bed."

She looked up into the Marquis' face as she spoke and something in his expression made her heart start beating wildly. Without realising what she was doing, she turned and walked across to the window to the open casement.

She did not see the beauty of the setting sun or the white wash of the waves as they splashed against the rocks below. Instead she was vividly conscious that the

Marquis had followed her and was standing just behind her.

After a moment he asked:

"Why have you been crying?"

She was surprised that he should be so perceptive as to notice the traces of the tears which she hoped she had washed away.

For a moment she could not think of an answer to his question and then as she realised he was waiting for her reply, she said hesitatingly.

"I . . . was . . . tired."

"I can understand that," he said in his deep voice. "And do you perhaps also feel a little sad that the adventure is over? Do you regret the thrill and excitement of knowing that, however dangerous and uncomfortable it was, we were outwitting the enemy, and confounding the French soldiers who were searching for us?"

"Y . . . Yes," Lucretia murmured.

"I do not have to tell you," the Marquis went on, "how wonderful you were! I did not know a woman could be so brave, so uncomplaining, so valiant, so utterly and completely magnificent!"

She felt herself quiver at the warmth of his words.

"D. . .do. . .y. . .you really mean. . .th. . .hhat?" hat?" she stammered.

"I mean it—and so much more," he answered.

"I am . . . humiliated that I . . . collapsed at the . . . end."

"Do you not think that I have cursed myself for being insensitive enough to drive you so hard?" the Marquis asked. "In my anxiety to get you away safely, Lucretia, I forgot how small and frail you are. I was brutal in what I asked of you."

Lucretia could not answer him. She could only feel the tears flooding into her eyes because he was speaking so kindly.

"It will be a thrilling tale," the Marquis went on, "to tell our children and our grandchildren! But there is one question that I feel sure they will ask and which I want to ask you first."

191

"What is . . . that?" Lucretia tried to say, but the words would not come.

"I want to know the real reason why you came after me," the Marquis said. "Why you worried that first night in the wood in case I should get cold? Why you were anxious about my hand, and why when we were both so hungry you gave me a great deal more than my fair share of the omelette?"

His voice died away, and because there had been a note in it which she had never heard before, Lucretia found herself trembling.

She felt she was going to burst into tears, and she held onto the window-sill fighting for self-control.

"Look at me, Lucretia!" the Marquis said.

She knew that she dared not do so, and after a moment when she had not turned he said:

"So disobedient! Yet it was only a very few days ago that you promised to obey me! 'To love, honour and obey'—those were the words you said when we were married. But now you will not obey me, and there is no reason why you should honour me. So that leaves only one other thing—love."

The word seemed to vibrate between them.

"Did you marry me for my title, Lucretia?"

The question was so unexpected that without thinking, without even hesitating, she retorted:

"No, of course not! Do you imagine I would marry any man unless . . ."

She stopped suddenly. She realised that the Marquis had caught her off her guard and she saw the pit into which she had fallen so easily.

She shut her eyes.

"Now I have nothing left," she thought, "not even pride."

". . . unless you loved him," the Marquis said: finishing her sentence.

There was silence for a moment before he said:

"Look at me, Lucretia, I have something to tell you."

The words were a command and Lucretia felt it was useless to fight any longer. She had lost the last battle,

192

and she turned towards him feeling he had taken even her will away.

The Marquis looked down at her pale, unhappy little face, at her eyes filled with unshed tears, at the trembling of her lips. Then he said very quietly:

"I want to say to you, Lucretia, something which I swear before God I have never said to any other woman in my life—I love you!"

For a moment she thought she must be mistaken in what she had heard and she did not understand.

Then he saw the life come into her face and a dazzling light to her eyes, before with a little inarticulate murmur she moved instinctively towards him and hid her face against his shoulder.

His arms went round her holding her very close.

"I love you, my precious one. I love you more than I believed it possible ever to love a woman."

"Is . . . that . . . really . . . true?"

She could only whisper the words. She thought she must be dreaming.

"It is true—I love you!"

"But . . . you hate . . . unfledged . . . girls."

He gave a little laugh that was very tender.

"So that was the reason for that brilliant, intelligent, almost convincing performance which left me curious and very intrigued!"

"Did you . . . guess it was a . . . p . . . pretence?" Lucretia asked, her face still hidden.

"Not at first," the Marquis answered. "But as an expert in the art of disguise, Lucretia, I must tell you that you forgot one very important item."

"What was . . . that?"

"You forgot to disguise your eyes."

"How . . . could . . . I?" she enquired.

"You could not prevent them being very unsophisticated, very innocent and very young!" the Marquis told her. "And there was something else which surprised me, my darling."

"And what was . . . that?"

"When in the barn I silenced your mouth with mine because I knew there was someone listening to us down below, I was convinced against all reason that I was the first man who had ever touched your lips."

He felt Lucretia quiver against him. Then putting, his fingers under her chin, he turned her face up to his.

"Shall I find out if that was the truth?" he asked and his voice was hoarse.

The tears from her eyes had run down her cheeks. Very gently he kissed them away before he kissed her eyes and then the corners of her mouth one after the other, until as her lips trembled and she wanted more than she had ever wanted anything in her whole life to feel the touch of his, he kissed her.

She felt again the wild ecstasy which she had felt when he first kissed her in the barn, shoot through her like a shaft of lightening.

But now it was more intense, more wonderful, more rapturous, until as her lips clung to his she could feel a strange flame awaken within her and seer its way through her body.

When finally the Marquis raised his head he knew he had never seen a woman's face so radiant.

"My beautiful darling," he said unsteadily, "my brave, sweet, perfect little wife!"

The deep note in his voice made her once again turn her face away because she felt so shy.

"Was ... that more ... experienced?" she whispered.

He smiled, his lips against her hair.

"It was more wonderful than any kiss I have ever known," he answered. "But I shall have to explain to you, my beloved, that while a man likes a sophisticated woman to amuse and entertain him he wants his wife to be pure and untouched—except by him."

His arms tightened and he said harshly:

"I would want to kill any man who had touched you in the past, and I swear I will murder anyone who attempts to do so in the future."

He held her closer still and added:

"What is more, my sweet, you are mine, and if I catch you looking under your eyelashes in that provocative manner at any man except me—I will beat you!"

194

She quivered at his masterfulness and he said with difficulty:

"Before I kiss you again, my darling, I want to tell you our plans while I can still remember them. I thought, if you agree, we would stay here for a little while and then we will sail slowly back along the coast to Dover.

"The Prime Minister has asked me to investigate the smuggling activities which are assuming alarming proportions, because it means that Napoleon is gaining our gold with which to pursue his war."

Lucretia raised her head quickly from his shoulder.

"It will ... not be ... dangerous?" she asked.

"No," the Marquis answered, "I am only to investigate their activities—not to stop or apprehend them. That will be the job of the military."

He saw the fear fade from her eyes and added:

"But if I am in danger, I shall have you with me to protect me!"

She gave a little choked laugh and he went on:

"And after that I thought we might spend the summer together at Merlyncourt."

He saw her eyes widen with delight and added softly:

"You will not be outside the gates any longer, my darling, you will be inside with me. There will be so much for us to do. Especially we will want to put the treasures your father has given me back in their rightful places."

"I would ... love to do ... that and to be at Merlyncourt," Lucretia answered, "if it ... will not ... bore you."

"Do you really think I could be bored with you?" the Marquis asked. "I am in love my darling and never again when we are together need you be afraid of having a bored bridegroom."

He kissed her cheek his lips lingering on her soft skin before he said.

"Together! that is the important word, and we will also be together at night. So there will be no question of your being lonely or needing a telescope!"

His arms tightened around her and he added very quietly:

"Nor shall we need a pillow between us."

"You . . . took it away," Lucretia said accusingly.

"Yes, I removed it," he answered. "You were so warm, soft and adorable I longed to have you close to me."

"Why did you not . . . tell me?" Lucretia asked. "I thought you did not . . . want me. You never said . . . anything to make me think you did . . . all the time we were in France . . . together. You never . . . kissed me. I thought when I awoke . . . this morning that I had . . . lost you . . . completely."

"You could never do that, my precious," the Marquis answered, "and if you only knew how hard it was for me not to touch you, not to kiss you."

He paused as he felt her quiver at his words, before he continued.

"I was afraid of frightening you when we were alone, and I was not certain if you loved me! But it was very difficult not to tell you that you were the most beautiful person I have ever seen!"

"Do . . . you mean . . . that?"

"You are more beautiful than I believed it possible for a woman to be," he answered. "When you first reminded me of the Madonnas in the early Italian paintings, I had a feeling then that I had discovered something so unique, so wonderful that it was what I had been searching for all my life. But when you teased and provoked me, I was afraid."

"Afraid?"

"That other men had loved you before me," the Marquis replied.

"And would that have . . . mattered . . . very much?"

He held her so close she could hardly breathe.

"It would have mattered to me," he answered. "I wanted you to belong to me, to be mine alone and not promiscuous like all the women I had known before."

Lucretia's eyes were looking into his and he said tenderly:

"When those drunken brutes insulted you and you

did not understand what they asked, I knew you were only a child and at the same time the woman I had idealised in my heart."

"Is this really . . . happening?" Lucretia asked, "did you say . . . that you . . . loved me?"

It was like the cry of a child who wants to be re-assured.

"I love you with all my heart and with all my soul," the Marquis answered. "That is what I advised you, Lucretia, to ask of any man who wished to make love with you, and that is what—I offer you."

She drew a deep breath and he said:

"When we were in bed together at the farm, and last night when I undressed you, and thought you were the most exquisite thing I had ever seen in my life, I behaved, as I promised you I would, like a gentleman!"

He paused before he continued softly.

"But Lucretia, I am very bored with behaving like—a gentleman."

The Marquis waited for Lucretia's reply. Then with the colour rising in her cheeks and lowering her eyes because she was shy, she murmured so he could only just hear:

"I would not . . . wish you to be . . . bored . . . My Lord."

He gave a sound that was half a cry of triumph and half a laugh of sheer happiness. Then he was holding her close against his heart and taking the pins from her hair so that it fell over her shoulders reaching to below her waist.

"You are so lovely, my darling," he said hoarsely, "I want to kiss you from the top of your violet-scented head to the soles of your poor sore little feet. But for the moment I can go no further than the irresistible softness of your lips because they entice me as no woman's lips have ever done!"

As he spoke he pulled her dress from her white shoulder and his lips were on the rounded perfection of her neck. It reminded him of the swans at Merlyncourt.

Then as his hand caressed her small tip-tilted breast

so that she quivered with a strange feeling she had never known before, his lips found hers.

They clung together with a rapture and a joy which as he drew her closer and closer against him was almost past thought.

"I love you, God, how I love you!" the Marquis cried.

Lucretia looked into his eyes. She saw there the same expression which had left her shaken and breathless when she had knelt at his feet to remove his boots.

It was love!

A love overwhelming, demanding, possessive, and burning so fiercely with the fire of passion that for a second she shrank from it lest it consumed her utterly.

It was not the gentle comfortable emotion she had expected. It was violent, powerful, tempestuous and it was what she would experience when she 'made love' with the man she loved and who loved her!

"You are mine!" the Marquis said as he drew her closer and still closer. "Mine and I worship you. You are my only love, my wife and my whole life."

Lucretia felt his heart beating frantically against hers and she thrilled with an excitement which was almost unbearable in its intensity.

Then she knew that this was the wonder, the beauty and the glory of the divine ecstasy which he had told her would carry them both towards the heart of the sun.

"I love . . . you . . . too," she whispered against the Marquis's lips and there was no more need for words.

ABOUT THE AUTHOR

BARBARA CARTLAND, the celebrated romantic author, historian, playwright, lecturer, political speaker and television personality, has now written over 150 books. Miss Cartland has had a number of historical books published and several biographical ones, including that of her brother, Major Ronald Cartland, who was the first Member of Parliament to be killed in the War. This book had a foreword by Sir Winston Churchill.

In private life, Barbara Cartland, who is a Dame of the Order of St. John of Jerusalem, has fought for better conditions and salaries for Midwives and Nurses. As President of the Royal College of Midwives (Hertfordshire Branch), she has been invested with the first Badge of Office ever given in Great Britain, which was subscribed to by the Midwives themselves. She has also championed the cause for old people and founded the first Romany Gypsy Camp in the world.

Barbara Cartland is deeply interested in Vitamin Therapy and is President of the British National Association for Health.

Barbara Cartland

The world's bestselling author of romantic fiction. Her stories are always captivating tales of intrigue, adventure and love.